Dedication

This book is dedicated in memory of my parents, Louis and Genevieve Wilczenski, the two most important mentors, coaches and supervisors in my life.
FLW

To Gladys Barr Harper, an elementary school teacher from 1920 to 1970. She was indeed a mentor, coach and supervisor to thousands of children and colleagues, including her granddaughter, Rebecca A. Schumacher.
RAS

To my husband, Gianluca, for all the support and encouragement he provided to me as I wrote this book and we looked forward to the birth of our son, Matteo!
ALC

Table of Contents

Preface

"School Counseling Principles: Mentoring and Supervising" addresses the need to develop expertise among school counselors for the roles of mentor and supervisor as the American School Counselor Association (ASCA) implements the ASCA National Model and adopts new training standards for graduate education. The ASCA National Model describes a multi-faceted role for school counselors, including those of leader and change agent. These new roles are too complex for school counselor education programs to adequately address during the relatively brief graduate training. Mentoring and supervising are necessary during the critical induction period for novice school counselors and throughout the professional lifespan, ensuring practitioners are knowledgeable about current reform efforts and keeping them abreast of the latest developments in the field. Sustained professional development reinforces the importance of a strong professional identity among school counselors. The support and learning opportunities provided through mentoring and supervisory relationships may reduce burnout and promote job satisfaction.

School counselors typically view themselves as mentors or supervisors when they interact with graduate students in practicum and internship, and when assuming leadership positions. In addition, many school counselors informally seek mentoring or supervision from their peers.

Because mentoring and supervising are not mandated, chances are high that a school counselor functioning in a mentor/supervisor role has not received any training for those roles. Yet school counselors need regular feedback to ensure they provide appropriate and effective programs and services. Improved mentoring and supervisory practices in school counseling will benefit the profession, and consequently, the schools and students we serve.

Several premises underlie the conceptual framework for this book:

1. School counseling mentors/supervisors adhere to the same ethical principles as all school counselors as outlined in the ASCA ethical codes regarding the student as the primary client.
2. Mentoring and supervisory decisions should be data-based to provide evidence for practices.
3. Effective mentoring/supervision requires knowledge of methods and models, interpersonal sensitivity, communicative abilities and technical skills.

"School Counseling Principles: Mentoring and Supervising" is an essential American School Counselor Association publication in this era of educational and school counseling reform. The principles reviewed in this volume apply whether one is mentoring or supervising K-12 students, school counseling interns, novice school counselors or seasoned professionals. This book focuses on why and how mentoring and supervisory relationships are beneficial to personal and professional growth. It provides practical guidelines explaining the "how-to" of mentoring and supervising for school counselors at all career stages. Included as well are numerous case studies, discussion questions, training exercises, forms and resources for professional development. The book is appropriate for professional preparation courses for school counselor practitioners and school counselor educators. Mentoring and supervising are critical leadership development roles promoting ASCA's unified vision of school counseling.

Although tasks performed by mentors and supervisors typically overlap, the two sections of the book emphasize the skills each role requires:

- *Section I* explains how mentoring helps protégés with the subjective aspects of the school counselor in a school environment (e.g., navigating effectively through the system).
- *Section II* demonstrates how supervision facilitates personal and professional development.

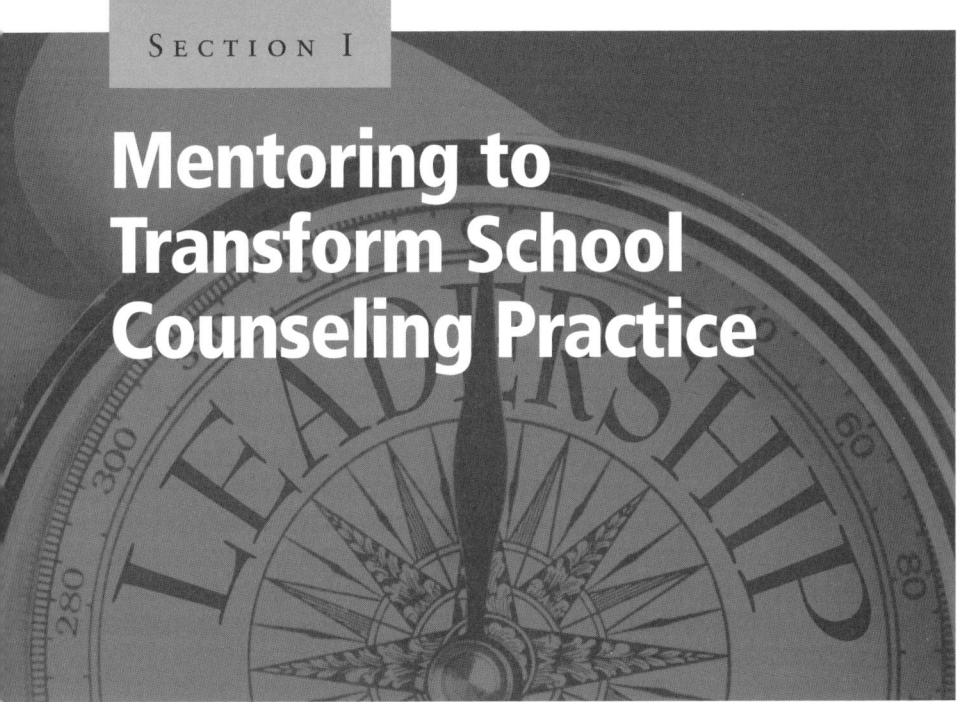

Mentoring to Transform School Counseling Practice

For centuries it has been said that almost always, wherever independence and creativity flourish and persist and important creative achievements occur, there is some other person who plays the role of mentor, sponsor, patron or guru.

— E. PAUL TORRANCE (1984, P.1)

Origins of mentoring

The term "mentor" probably originated from Homer's epic, "The Odyssey." When the Ulysses embarked on his journey, he left his son, Telemachus, in the care of a servant, Mentor. It was Mentor who acted as the young man's teacher, advisor, friend and surrogate father. Rather than teaching Telemachus the skills he would need to win battles, Mentor's role was to teach Telemachus the values he would need to successfully rule Ithaca. The modern use of the term mentor can be traced to the protagonist in a book titled, "*Les Aventures de Telemaque*," (The Adventures of Telemachus) published in 1699 by Francois Fenelon (Roberts, 1999). Fenelon was appointed by Louis XIV to promote the character formation of his son, the Duke of Burgundy, who was second in line for the throne of France. He wrote this book as a guide for his young protégé.

For centuries, mentoring has been a way of transmitting customs, fostering talent and developing leadership. Examples of historical systems of mentorship include the guru tradition in Hinduism and Buddhism, as well as discipleships practiced in Judaism and Christianity.

Mentoring matters

A good example of mentoring is the extraordinary relationship between Charles Darwin and Professor John Henslow. Henslow imparted his knowledge and skills to Darwin, recommended Darwin for the Beagle voyage, cared for his specimens for five years as Darwin traveled around the world and supported his famous protégé at the origin-of-the-species trial. Darwin himself felt that his relationship with Henslow influenced his career more than any other circumstance (Darwin/Barlow, 1958). According to Nora Barlow, Darwin's granddaughter, Henslow helped Darwin "attain the faith in his aims and in himself which his boyhood at Shrewsbury had failed to provide" (1967, p. 7). In analyzing this mentoring relationship, McGreevy (1990) noted that Henslow gave Darwin the direction he needed at critical points in his life. As time when on, however, Darwin surpassed his mentor intellectually and could no longer discuss his theories with Henslow for fear of offending him. Had Henslow been a more competitive or ambitious man, perhaps the mentorship might have been impossible.

Definition

Today mentors provide their expertise to less-experienced individuals to help them advance their careers, enhance their education, and build their professional networks. Mentoring and counseling are related and can be applied to one another (Schweibert, 2000). Furthermore, a mentor is defined as a trusted counselor (see *www.merriam-webster.com/dictionary/ mentor*). The term "mentorship refers to a developmental relationship between a more-experienced mentor providing a less-experienced partner or protégé both support and opportunities for growth (Leonard & Hilgert, 2004).

Although definitions of mentoring vary somewhat, it is generally agreed that mentoring is a form of professional and organizational socialization. From their review of the literature, Lazovsky and Shimoni (2007) discovered consensus regarding five components of mentoring:

1. Mentoring is a helping relationship, primarily assisting the protégé in achieving long-term, broad goals.

2. Mentoring can consist of emotional support, role modeling, direct career assistance and professional development.
3. Mentoring is reciprocal, benefiting both parties.
4. Mentoring relationships are personal, requiring interaction between mentor and protégé.
5. Compared with their protégés, mentors show greater experience, influence and achievements within the mentoring setting.

Mentoring vs. supervising

Mentoring and supervising relationships are working alliances. As such, can mentors supervise their protégés? Yes, in the sense that a mentor must have good supervising skills to facilitate a protégé's professional growth. No, because protégés may be reluctant to share with their supervisors their personal concerns or areas where they need improvement.

How to choose and when to use each technique

Mentoring and supervising share similar goals of improving a protégé's performance. Mentors also supervise the performance of a protégé, providing constructive feedback and guiding professional development. Although mentoring is sometimes used as an umbrella term encompassing supervising, the two techniques are distinct.

Supervising involves evaluating and giving specific feedback to reinforce the desired performance. The evaluation of a supervisor may serve as the basis to formulate mentoring goals and objectives. Even though mentoring involves supervising, it goes above and beyond that to encourage the protégé to take on tasks and perform in a way that exceeds the job description or expectations.

In school counseling, a supervisor would be in a position to assess the protégé's performance and would be ethically responsible for the welfare of the students with whom the counselor worked. A mentor would help a protégé with the subjective aspects of counseling in a school environment; e.g., effectively navigating through the system.

Mentoring and school counseling

More than a quarter century ago, Boyd and Walker (1975) compared a school counselor's career to a cactus because "both survive on a minimum of nutrients from the environment" (p.103). Many counselors are isolated in their work, serving alone in one or more schools (Lund, 1990; Smith, 2000). For school counselors, there are no classrooms or set schedules. Because their activities are usually unseen, there is no clear public perception of the profession of school counseling. Administrators are typically the primary references for shaping a school counselor's identity (Matthes, 1992), and as a consequence, they often drift into quasi-administrative roles (Myrick, 1993). School counselors are frequently supervised by practitioners with little or no training in the field and with different professional priorities. Despite the ASCA National Model, there is often a disconnection between the role the profession recommends and the actual work of school counselors. These issues point to the critical need for leadership development roles in school counseling.

Progressive mentoring

For today's novice school counselors, their induction into the field is often a sink-or-swim process (Desmond, West, & Bubenzer, 2007). They may be quickly disillusioned when their graduate training does not prepare them to respond to multiple contingencies and ambiguous situations. Owens, Pernice-Duca, and Thomas (2009) reported the results of a survey indicating high school counselors often felt the need for supplemental training beyond graduate school to address a variety of issues surfacing in their practices. Although they have been socialized into the profession, newly minted school counselors must be socialized into the organization in which they are employed. A pilot study by Armstrong, Balkin, Long and Caldwell (2006) revealed how mentoring supported elementary-level school counselors and helped them survive the first year on the job. Novice school counselors in that study indicated an increase in self-efficacy as a result of the mentoring program. School counselor education programs and school districts need to be sensitized to developmental challenges faced by early career school counselors as well as to the needs of more seasoned practitioners.

A progressive mentoring model should be planned for successive career stages. Veteran counselors also require assistance as they encounter increasingly complex problems in schools. Mentoring provides a needed support system and professional development opportunity for both novices and veteran school counselors. In addition, inter-professional mentoring can extend the school counseling program's resources and reach. The transformed role for school counselors is to provide leadership in educational reform. It can be achieved by school counselors mentoring administrators and teachers to collaboratively meet their mutual goals for students.

School counselor retention

Although information regarding the cost effectiveness of mentoring programs as a retention strategy for school counselors is not available, such data have been collected concerning teacher mentor programs. For example, "The total cost of [teacher] turnover in the Chicago Public Schools is estimated to be over $86 million per year" (Barnes, Crowe, & Schaefer, 2007). Through recruiting, hiring, processing, and training costs, "… schools lose $17,872 on every teacher who leaves the district. By implementing an effective retention strategy, such as a high-quality induction program at a cost of $6,000 per teacher per year, Chicago could reduce teacher turnover and save millions of dollars." Similar findings regarding the costs of turnover and benefits of mentoring programs might be expected for school counselors.

The Massachusetts School Counselor Association (MASCA) recognized the need for a formal induction program for novice school counselors and is addressing that need through the state professional organization. The MASCA's governing board initiated an Emerging Leaders Program in 2007 to include a mentoring program and workshops for new school counselors. Although retention data are not available, anecdotal feedback from participants over the past three years has been uniformly positive (R. Bardwell, personal communication, April 28, 2009; MASCA, 2009).

Mentoring for social justice

Many school counselors are familiar with youth-mentoring programs designed to encourage academic and social engagement through peer- and adult-volunteer support. The goals are to provide a source of encouragement to students at risk for school failure. Because the mentoring experience benefits both the mentor and protégé, this service provides a rich learning opportunity and source of personal satisfaction.

A major problem with the educational system in the U.S. is the inequity in academic achievement and educational opportunity across racial, ethnic and socio-economic groups. Gaps are evident in high school graduation rates, college attendance, advanced placement course enrollments, standardized test results for minorities (except Asian Americans) and low-income students. In their roles as academic advisors, school counselors bear some responsibility for creating and maintaining achievement and opportunity gaps. Novice school counselors need to be made aware of how societal structures privilege some groups and perpetuate inequities for others. Mentors will play a key role in preparing their protégés to grapple with social justice issues.

Holcomb-McCoy (2007) defined social justice as "… the way in which human rights are manifested in the everyday lives of people at every level of society" (p.17). Lee Bemak and Chung (2005) as well as others (Holcomb-McCoy, 2007; Lee, 2005) emphasized that traditional school counseling must be transformed to address issues of social justice. A social justice orientation in school counseling acknowledges the role of the dominant culture in dictating educational success and failure. School counseling mentors need to help their protégés understand how all types of oppression (e.g., racism, classism, ableism, sexism, lookism) adversely affect the social and emotional well-being of students which in turn, interferes with their academic achievement. Protégés need to recognize how this oppression is internalized and reinforced through traditional school counseling practices. Mentors should promote school counseling focusing on the strengths of students (e.g., resourceful, tenacious) to counter negative effects of marginalization and stigmatizing labels (e.g., oppositional, unmotivated).

EXERCISE:

A teacher in your school states that all children who live in a certain low-income housing project are doomed for school failure and drop out. Identify strategies you would use to challenge a bias a colleague may not recognize.

Informal and formal mentoring relationships

Mentoring relationships can be informal or formal. Informal relationships develop on their own as friendships between colleagues. Formal mentoring is an assigned relationship often involving training for mentors and protégés as well as a series of regularly scheduled meetings. Some professions have structured induction programs whereby new hires (protégés) are paired with more experienced people (mentors) to acquire information, observe good role models and obtain advice about career advancement. In other cases, mentoring is used to groom early career employees identified as having high potential for moving into leadership roles (the protégé is paired with a senior-level mentor for a series of meetings about professional development). A similar method of high-potential mentoring is to place the protégé in a series of jobs in different areas of an organization (all for short periods of time) in anticipation of learning the organization's structure, culture and methods. The new employees paired with mentors are twice as likely to remain in their jobs as those who do not get mentoring (Kaye & Jordan-Evans, 2005). Although mentorship usually involves face-to-face interactions, mentoring in cyberspace (e-mentoring; virtual mentoring), with its ability to overcome barriers of time and distance, is gaining popularity (Bierema & Merriam, 2002).

Cross-cultural mentoring relationships

Cross-cultural mentoring can be both enriched and complicated in diverse settings. Professional development literature frequently cites mentoring as one of the few common characteristics of a successful career, particularly for women and minorities.

Developing mentorships across gender and racial lines is a challenge facing many women and minorities. In those situations, power differentials between mentors and protégés are more complex. Because it may be difficult to find a mentor from a similar cultural background (including gender, sexual orientation, race/ethnicity, disability/ability status, and socioeconomic status) it can be challenging for protégés to experience a positive mentoring relationship. This is particularly salient when the protégé is part of an underrepresented group within the organization (Benishek, Bieschke, Park, & Slattery, 2004). In addition, there are many obstacles to forming cross-gender or cross-cultural mentorships including stereotypes, tokenism and concerns about public appearance. More specifically, in reviewing the literature Benishek and colleagues found that in some cases male mentors have perceived limitations in their female protégés' work performance, doubting their professional abilities and goals. In addition, these cross-gender mentoring relationships may be colored with sexual innuendos or may be perceived as such by other employees within the organization. As a result, female protégés may not be presented with equivalent career opportunities as their male counterparts. However, researchers have found that when women are mentored by men, they tended to receive higher salaries due to the male mentor's status position within the organization (Walker, 2006; Benishek et al.).

Similarly, there can be challenges in experiencing a positive mentorship if mentor and protégé are from different cultural backgrounds. Developing trust in cross-cultural mentoring relationships can take longer due to external factors such as societal norms and racial/ethnic tensions. These external influences can result in greater disparities in power than would ordinarily exist in mentoring relationships between individuals from similar gender and cultural backgrounds (Johnson-Bailey & Cervero, 2004). Furthermore, institutional culture, levels of awareness and racial self-identities of protégé and mentor affect the mentoring relationship (Barker, 2007). Specifically, in work settings characterized by hegemonic organizational structures, protégés and mentors encounter significant obstacles to negotiating successfully the inherent power differentials within the institution and within the mentoring relationship (Hansman, 2001, June). With regard to racial/ethnic identity development, mentors and protégés may not share similar awareness levels of racial/ethnic self-identity. If that is the case, a beneficial, open discussion of cultural differences in the mentoring relationship may not occur.

To address these added complexities often present in cross-gender and cross-cultural mentoring relationships, researchers have recommended several strategies. First, it is important to recognize and understand differences in life experiences between mentor and protégé, and to value the contributions protégés bring to the relationship (Benishek et al., 2004; Ambrose, 2003). For example, often the focus is on what protégé achieves from the mentoring relationship. However, the mentor benefits by personal growth, by earning respect within the institution and by developing greater sensitivity toward individuals from diverse backgrounds (Johnson-Bailey & Cervero, 2004). Furthermore, the protégé offers a unique perspective, helping the mentor identify previously unconsidered, possible alternatives (Benishek et al.). In a school setting, this approach benefits all parties involved, including students, parents, teachers and other support staff.

Second, mentors should facilitate an open and honest dialogue addressing complexities inherent in cross-gender and cross-cultural mentoring relationships (Barker, 2007; Johnson-Bailey & Cervero, 2004). More specifically, mentors should consider and discuss the mentoring relationship vis-à-vis the school's norms (and not solely the relationship itself). In some cases, the mentor and protégé experience differently the same work environment. Failure to address this discrepancy can complicate the mentoring relationship.

Third, mentors should acknowledge the presence of racism and discrimination (Johnson-Bailey & Cervero, 2004). Through increased cultural awareness, mentors can collaborate with protégés to achieve social justice and systemic change within school environments when the presence of institutional discrimination exists.

In planning and establishing effective diversity-focused mentoring programs, researchers have examined the effects of different mentoring models. Walker (2006) found relational models of mentoring are preferred over traditional models. The relationship model emphasizes the relationship, and therefore sensitivity to differences can be cultivated instead of following traditional hierarchical and directive mentoring practices. To facilitate the development of a trusting mentoring relationship, whenever possible it is helpful to engage in mentoring relationships with individuals who share a similar vision and life outlook (Johnson-Bailey & Cervero, 2004).

As an alternative to the relational model of mentoring, Benishek and colleagues (2004) recommend using a feminist mentoring model, which focuses on both the relational component and differences in power. The feminist mentoring framework encourages mentors to talk about multicultural issues, even if there appears to be little difference between mentor and protégé. This is because protégés could be part of a minority group in which differences are not observable, such as GLBT individuals, persons with disabilities and religious minorities. However, it behooves mentors to consider the protégé's level of identity development when determining the appropriate time to discuss issues of diversity (Benishek et al.).

When implementing formal mentoring programs for individuals from marginalized groups, Hansman (2001) identified the possibility that such mentoring relationships can inadvertently serve to further perpetuate current hegemonic organizational practices. Rather than helping to encourage the promotion of minorities within the institution, formal mentoring programs can result in differential treatment of employees. However, formal mentoring programs can often provide opportunities for minority groups when mentors and protégés are empowered to bridge institutional gaps and challenge rigid power differences within the organization (Hansman). Formal mentoring programs tend to be more successful in this regard when top leadership supports diversity initiatives (Ambrose, 2003). When planning and implementing formal mentoring programs in school districts, it is important to garner support from the major stakeholders involved, including support personnel, teachers, school administrators and parents/guardians.

Because mentoring is a two-way activity, protégés often look for someone who is "like" them. Establishing an effective mentorship across gender and racial lines requires a willingness on both sides to engage in a trusting and empowering relationship (Harvard Business Essentials, 2004).

EXERCISE:

What values guide you as a mentor? What assumptions about mentoring do you take for granted?

Technology and mentoring

The first use of technology for mentoring was telementoring, using telephone communication. It was replaced with e-mentoring with the advent of the Internet. The term "e-mentoring" means to establish and maintain a mentorship using e-mail or online software. Early e-mentoring programs primarily used e-mail to connect mentors and protégés. However, confidentiality is an issue with e-mail because messages can be forwarded, blind-copied, or read by someone other than the intended recipient. Now e-mentoring tends to be Web-based, offering the benefit of secure, password-protected sites for both parties.

There are advantages and disadvantages to e-mentoring. It overcomes the barriers of time and distance, and thus can facilitate relationship building between busy colleagues who may be assigned to different schools within a district. Unfortunately, the medium does not transmit the extra information carried in visual cues, such as facial expressions, that can clarify the meaning of verbal messages. Furthermore, there is evidence that people interpret social and emotional information differently depending on the medium (Coomey & Wilczenski, 2005). In fact, to avoid misinterpreting text-based messages, emoticons are often used to convey the affective content of e-mail communication. Telementoring continues to be used as a backup or supplement to e-mentoring. Vocal chats (e.g., *Wimba*) or video conferencing provide more communicative information, but those systems are more costly, and at present, are not as widely accessible as e-mail and the telephone.

An example of a formal electronic mentoring program is *e-Mentoring for Student Success* (eMSS), an online support system working in all 50 states to match new teachers with experienced mentor teachers (see *www.newteachercenter.org/eMISS/index.php*).

The program addresses professional development needs of both mentors and protégés through one-to-one and group online-meeting formats. It is easier to arrange in cyberspace and in face-to-face meetings collaborative partnerships across schools, school districts and universities. Because the e-mentoring program is asynchronous, participants can log on at their own convenience to find support for their work. For these reasons, eMSS may serve as a model for online mentoring in school counseling.

Mutual mentoring

Mentoring is typically defined as a top-down, one-to-one relationship with an experienced employee guiding and supporting the career development of a new hire or early career employee. "Mutual mentoring" differs from the traditional model by encouraging a broader, more flexible network of support that more closely mirrors real life situations in which no single person is expected to be all-knowing (University of Massachusetts Amherst, 2007). Within a mutual mentoring model, protégés build networks by engaging with multiple mentoring partners in non-hierarchical, collaborative and cross-cultural relationships to address specific areas of knowledge, skill and experience. These reciprocal relationships benefit not only the person known as a protégé in the traditional sense, but also the person traditionally known as the mentor. This mutuality can build a sense of community and a culture of mentoring where all members teach and learn from each other (Johnson, 2002). In fostering a culture of mutual mentoring, school counselors can turn to their peers within the same school setting, district-wide, or perhaps set up e-mentoring through state organizations. School counselors also may serve as mentors to teachers and administrators (and vice versa) as they work together for system change.

ACTIVITY

To link mentors and protégés in schools, speed mentoring might be tried as a networking strategy. Like speed dating, speed mentoring is a round-robin matchmaking process whereby mentors and protégés rotate to meet each other over a series of short 5- to 10-minute intervals. At the end of each interval, the organizer rings a bell or otherwise signals the participants to move on to the next meeting. First impressions are often lasting so mentors and protégés generally make quick decisions as to whether their professional interests are compatible. At the end of the speed mentoring session, both sets of participants submit a list of those with whom they would like further discussions. If there is a match, contact information is provided to the mentor and protégé.

Mentoring functions

Professional identity evolves over time. Although mentoring relationships are generally considered transitional at the early stage of induction into a career, sustained mentorships are important because the professional lifespan is longer today than in the past. People change job roles or switch career directions more frequently. Mentoring is especially important in a changing profession such as school counseling, which is undergoing a rapid and major transformation. There is a need for school counselor mentors who are knowledgeable about the current reform agendas of the American School Counselor Association (American School Counselor Association, 2003).

Mentors support protégés in expressing their ideas while protecting them from negative responses from peers and superiors. They inspire their protégés to realize their own goals by encouraging them to persevere despite obstacles and setbacks. A mentor not only trains the protégé to do the job well, but also shares experience, wisdom and political savvy by engaging in the following activities:

1. *Role modeling* – A mentor's behavior is a powerful model. A protégé observes and emulates how the mentor translates goals and values into practice.
2. *Culture brokering* – A mentor helps a protégé negotiate the organization socially and politically. The mentor clears the path or runs interference so the protégé can reach the appropriate contacts to achieve goals.

3. *Advocating* – A mentor champions the protégé's causes by trumpeting the protégé's work to influential others.

Personal characteristics of protégés and mentors

What characteristics of protégés and mentors make them effective partners? The relationship between the mentor and protégé is at the heart of mentoring. Certainly, good protégés have the prerequisite intelligence and technical skills for the job. In addition, they need to welcome feedback and be willing to assume responsibility for their own professional development. They need to accept challenges and be motivated to see each project through to a successful conclusion.

Effective mentors are competent in their profession and have strong interpersonal skills. They also need a network of contacts to help protégés access organizational resources. They give protégés the freedom to do things their own way. Good mentors must have the psychological competencies (or ego strength) to risk protégés' failures and to bolster their self-confidence by helping protégés overcome failures. Mentors must be so satisfied with their own lives and careers that they are always generous in their willingness to promote and to appropriately credit the protégé's work, thus advancing the protégé's standing within the organization.

Mentoring the mentor

School-based mentors are generally not trained for the role. Their mentoring work is based mainly on their personal traits and good will. Yet mentoring skills can be taught. Peace (1995) found that serving as a mentor enhanced the professional development of mentors themselves.

As school counselors are asked to be educational leaders and school change agents, mentoring for those roles has become a professional development challenge (DeVoss & Andrews, 2006). Mentoring programs can be a cost-effective professional development alternative to expensive seminars and university courses. Janas (1996) pointed out several considerations when initiating mentoring programs:

1. Selecting the mentor
2. Matching the mentor with a protégé
3. Setting goals and clarifying expectations
4. Establishing the mentor program

First, the mentor must possess the willingness, expertise and time to provide assistance to a protégé. School counselors usually acquire training in key mentoring skills such as active listening, relationship building, conflict resolution and problem solving through their graduate programs. In pairing mentors and protégés, the logistical issue of accessibility is important. The mentor/protégé pair must be able to contact each other in either face-to-face meetings or via electronic means (with cautions about confidentiality when using the Internet). Also, matching people of similar gender or cultural background may be important in some mentorships while not an issue in others. Mentors and protégés will need to decide what is to be accomplished through the relationship. A source of continual support (perhaps by school administration) will need to be provided for the mentor as he or she, in turn, provides support for the protégé. School professionals may leave their field because of limited opportunities for advancement (Wilczenski, 1997). Mentoring can help to increase a school counselor's influence and increasing variety in job tasks might lead to greater career satisfaction.

EXERCISE:

With your protégé's permission, tape record a mentoring session. Then transcribe and analyze the tape for content and process. What have you learned about your mentoring communication skills?

Training the protégé

Traditionally, mentoring programs have focused on training mentors rather than protégés. Yet the value of mentoring may rise with the increasing competence of the protégé. To benefit from mentoring, a protégé must acquire an understanding about that type of professional relationship. An effective mentor is aware of the different types of learning facing a protégé, facilitates each and thus enhancing the protégé's professional competence and further developing the mentorship. Evidence indicates mentoring dyads benefit when protégés are trained for their roles, when they know what to expect and how to take full advantage of the supportive relationship. In their study of mentor satisfaction, Kasprisin, Boyle-Single, Single, Ferrier, and Muller (2008) report mentors paired with trained protégés were more engaged in the relationship and held their protégés in higher esteem.

EXERCISE:

Review with your protégé specific situations when you delegated responsibility. Identify situations in which the protégé felt the tasks were delegated prematurely, as well as instances when you did not assign enough responsibility.

Learning school counseling by mentoring

Mentoring is more than teaching. Faculty may mentor graduate students by involving them in projects that go beyond typical class assignments, such as research and conference presentations. Often, faculty guide graduate students about negotiating with internship supervisors or about successful job interview strategies. Another way to prepare school counselors-in-training for future mentoring roles is to give them mentoring opportunities during their graduate education; acting as a mentor fosters and appreciation for the role. In addition, familiarity and experience with mentoring relationships may reduce anxiety about ultimately taking on that role as a professional.

As a pre-practicum assignment, graduate students enrolled in an introductory, professional school counseling course engage in service learning by mentoring at-risk first year undergraduate University students (Wilczenski & Coomey, 2007; Wilczenski & Schumacher, 2008). Goals of the mentoring including helping undergraduates negotiate the University, supporting them in making appropriate social and emotional adjustments to college life and advising them to seek academic assistance when necessary. This mentoring experience differs from other school counseling practicum placements or internships, as it extends the view of the school counselor-in-training to post-secondary education, giving students a deeper understanding of issues facing undergraduates as they enter college. As service-learning, the mentoring program addresses an authentic need to help undergraduates succeed their first year at the University. To promote reflection on their mentoring experiences, Suskind's book "A Hope in the Unseen" (1998/2005) is required reading in the introductory school counseling course.

Mentoring model

There are few models in counseling that specifically address mentoring. Tentoni (1995) proposed a paradigm for mentoring in counseling based on one developed for teacher education by Anderson and Shannon (1988). Three mentoring dispositions support the model: openness, leading by increment and expressing care and concern.

The model is centered on five mentoring domains and associated behaviors:

1. Teaching includes the behaviors of modeling, informing and defining.
2. Sponsoring includes protecting, supporting and promoting.
3. Encouraging includes affirming and inspiring.
4. Counseling includes listening, clarifying and advising.
5. Befriending includes accepting and relating.

Mentors should outline a mentoring plan by listing:

- Mentoring objectives
- Strategies to achieve the objectives
- Strategies to monitor progress
- Expected outcomes

Establishing a mentoring relationship

Research on mentoring has been conducted primarily in business and teacher education. A notable exception is the work in school counseling by Lazovsky and Shimoni (2007). They found that the match between the mentor and protégé is the linchpin of effective mentorships.

Mentors and protégés might begin the process of establishing a mentoring relationship by an honest appraisal of their own assets and liabilities:

- What are my personal strengths and weaknesses?
- How do I accept or give critical feedback?
- How positive is my outlook toward my life and career?
- Do I want to commit time and energy to a fairly long-term mentoring relationship?

Mentors need to assess their understanding of the process of mentoring:

- What do mentors do?
- How do mentoring relationships begin and end?
- What do I have to offer a protégé?
- What does it mean to be a role model?

Protégés need to think about what they want to gain from a mentorship:

- What are the qualities you value in a mentor?
- What behaviors or skills do you want to improve?
- Identify colleagues who have those qualities and skills.

Mentors and protégés need to identify their hopes for the mentoring relationship:

- What do I expect from this relationship?
- What am I willing to contribute to this relationship?
- How similar or different is my potential mentor or protégé from me?
- How much do those similarities or differences matter to me?

EXERCISE:

How can the likelihood of success of the mentor relationship be measured? In one column, the mentor lists the resources he or she is willing to give to the relationship (time, attention, knowledge, skills and political know-how). In a second column, list the protégé's developmental needs. Draw black lines to connect the mentor's competencies with the protégé's needs. Draw red lines to indicate those situations where the protégé would be better off with a different mentor. Of course, the more red lines, the less likely the pairing will be a productive one, due to a mismatch between the mentor's resources and the protégé's needs. The more links between them, the more likely the relationship will be productive.

Mentoring agreement

To summarize, mentors and protégés may need to sign an agreement considering the following elements:

1. *Relationship issues*
   - What should the mentor know about the protégé to enhance the mentorship?
   - What can the mentor do to increase the comfort level of the protégé?
2. *Expectations*
   - What is the most important thing that should be gained from the mentorship?
   - What are goals and expectations of the mentor and protégé?

- What support do you want to receive as the protégé?
- What support are you willing to provide as the mentor?

3. *Logistics*
   - How often will meetings be held?
   - What is the best way to communicate outside of regular meeting times (e-mail, phone or face-to-face visits)?
   - What are realistic time frames for responding to e-mails, returning calls, etc.?
   - How will credit be assigned on projects to which both mentor and protégé contributed?

Stages of mentoring relationships

Johnson (2007) described a predictable sequence of developmental stages in mentoring relationships that roughly parallel the developmental stages which occur in other professional relationships such as counseling and consultation:

1. Initiation: During the first stage of mentoring, the primary, relational task is for the mentor and protégé to engage in sufficient interactions to determine whether the mentorship has the potential to develop. During this entry stage, the relationship will most likely be viewed as positive if both mentor and protégé can see mutual benefits. Mentors need to keep in mind that protégés may be particularly vulnerable at this early stage as they embark on a new career or job role. Protégés may be struggling to assimilate new identities or anxious about their success in a new pursuit.

2. Cultivation: This is the "investment" stage, as interpersonal bond tighten between the mentor and protégé, and when they test relationship expectations against reality. During this stage, mentors become invested in their protégé's success, offering them guidance to achieve career and personal goals.

3. Separation: A reduction in the intensity of the mentoring relationship characterizes this stage. As the protégé moves toward greater independence, the number of mentoring functions drops off and may possibly trigger range of emotional responses from mentors and protégés. Dependency, conflict, anger or sadness may surface about the changes in the relationship.

4. Redefinition: A mentorship connection may endure beyond the separation phase. This redefinition phase is characterized by less formality and less frequent interaction. The relationship moves toward a collegial friendship.

Mentoring rewards

Besides advancing the interests of the protégé, mentoring can benefit the mentor in several ways:

1. *Smoother learning curves for new employees.* Protégés learn the requirements of the job more quickly.
2. *Increased opportunities to communicate importance of organizational goals and values.* Protégés learn about the nature of collegiality and working relationships within the organization as well as the strategic importance of organizational goals and values.
3. *Employee loyalty and retention.* Although pay raises may not be possible, a supportive work environment and the achievement of career goals may provide sources of job satisfaction, thus reducing burnout and turnover.
4. *Additional source of information about the organization.* Protégés can increase a mentor's contacts throughout the organization, facilitating the flow of information and communication.
5. *Support for ideas and innovations.* Providing a safety zone for protégés to express their ideas can lead to a creative and vibrant work environment.
6. *Allies for the future.* As protégés advance in influence in the organization, they become key resources for the mentor's own work.
7. *More time.* Protégés can assist with projects that ultimately improve their skills while increasing the mentor's job efficiency.

Mentoring pitfalls

Although the benefits of mentoring are well-documented, mentoring relationships sometimes become dysfunctional. Mentorships are not immune from misunderstandings and conflict. Like all human relationships, mentoring can have its ups and downs. In their study of protégés, Eby and Allen (2002) reported negative mentoring experiences clustered into two factors: distancing/manipulative behavior and poor dyadic fit. These negative mentoring experiences had an adverse impact on the protégé job satisfaction and stress levels.

There are a few problems in mentoring indicating the relationship may need to be dissolved. Sometimes mentoring can inhibit a protégé's professional development rather than enhance it. It may be necessary to sever the relationship if a protégé becomes so dependent on the mentor that there is actually a decline in performance. Another reason to terminate a mentorship is if the protégé is not developing new skills or adapting to the work culture. Cross-gender mentoring can be misunderstood as an improper personal liaison and rumors may make the mentorship impossible. In these cases, other professional development techniques such as supervising may be more appropriate.

Other issues that arise in mentoring may be remedied. When either the mentor or protégé or both are not living up to expectations, it's time to clarify expectations. Perhaps the two should renegotiate the relationship in terms of time commitment, support for new projects, etc. Mentors should be careful that assignments for protégés are compatible with their skills, rather than overselling them for key positions. Colleagues may be jealous and accuse a mentor of favoritism if the protégé seems undeserving of a certain assignment or position. The opposite situation to a protégé receiving favorable treatment by a mentor is the case of protégé who receives from a mentor harsher feedback regarding job performance than do other colleagues.

When problems arise, a frank discussion between mentor and protégé may help to revitalize the relationship or to reach a mutual decision to dissolve it. The following questions may help to identify the issues:

- Are your needs being met?
- What could be done to improve the relationship?
- Are there particular issues that need to be addressed?
- Are we spending too much or too little time together?
- Do you feel another mentor would be better able to help you achieve your goals?

Assuming that issues about the mentorship are identified, the discussion questions can be repeated after a month to monitor progress. If the issues are not resolved, there would be justification terminate the mentoring partnership.

Sometimes a mentorship may reach a natural conclusion, and either the protégé or mentor can end the relationship. One reason a mentor may decide to terminate the mentorship is that the protégé has simply outgrown the mentor. Perhaps the protégé needs a mentor with a different set of skills to continue his or her professional development.

ETHICAL ISSUES: DO NO HARM

Mutual benefits imply mutual responsibility and accountability for the mentoring relationship. A mentoring relationship involves a hierarchy and power differential. Mentors and protégés should demonstrate and expect professional and ethical behavior (e.g., respecting boundaries and confidentiality). Mentors need to model those behaviors.

Part C.1 of the American School Counselor Association Ethical Standards for School Counselors addresses responsibilities to colleagues and professional relationships (ASCA, 2004). The professional school counselor:

C.1.a. Establishes and maintains professional relationships with faculty, staff and administration to facilitate an optimum counseling program.

C.1.b. Treats colleagues with professional respect, courtesy and fairness. The qualifications, views and findings of colleagues are represented to accurately reflect the image of competent professionals.

There are several ethical issues that apply specifically to the mentoring process:

- *Confidentiality* needs to be preserved. Remembering what is said by a protégé and what is learned from other sources can be difficult. Mentors need to be vigilant and not betray confidences.
- *Conflicts* of interest need to be declared openly. There may be instances where the protégé's best interest conflict with those of the mentor. The possible results of not being honest should be discussed at the start of the relationship.
- "Knowledge is *power*." By its very nature mentoring gives the mentor considerable knowledge about the protégé. The mentor is entrusted with this knowledge and cannot misuse it.
- *False expectations* should not be encouraged. After a relationship has been established, a protégé may expect more from the mentor than he or she is able or willing to give. It may appear that the mentor is letting down the protégé.

Designing and evaluating mentor programs

Although school counseling students demonstrate skill acquisition during graduate training, without ongoing support, the skills deteriorated within one year (Baker, Daniels, & Greely, 1990; Spooner & Stone, 1977). Increasing recognition of this need for ongoing support and professional development has led to recommendations to design mentor programs for school counselors (Agnew, Vaught, Getz, & Fortune, 2000; Peace & Sprinthall, 1998) with the ultimate goal of delivering effective school counseling services that facilitate student development.

The objectives of a mentor program to assist school counseling protégés are:

- to expand school counseling practices to conform to supervision;
- to develop problem-solving and counseling skills in the areas of academic, personal, social and career development; and
- to emphasize evidence-based practice by collecting data on the effectiveness of school counseling activities through measures of student learning outcomes.

VanZandt and Perry (1992) described a statewide-mentoring program in Maine to support new school counselors during their first year on the job. Based on their experiences, the authors made several recommendations for establishing a mentoring program:

- Promote mentoring as professionally enhancing and worthwhile.
- Do not rely exclusively on self-selected mentors; actively recruit able and experienced practitioners.
- Provide mentors a preparation package that explains the role in a way that affirms their professional knowledge and skills.
- Provide networks to expand beyond initial mentor-protégé pairings.
- Recognize mentors through some system of rewards or acknowledgement.

Peace (1995) created a school counselor mentor program in North Carolina using a cognitive-developmental perspective. The program focused on the developmental growth of veteran practitioners, who in turn fostered the development of novices. Professional development occurred through role play, modeling, reflection, independent practice, performance feedback and emotional support.

To answer the call for school counselor mentor programs, the state of Indiana, through its School Counselor Association, designed a mentor certification training program. The program provides mentoring support to novice school counselors during their first two years of employment. It grants professional development credits and pays a small stipend to mentors. The program consists of learning the Standards for School Counseling Professionals, understanding the role of the mentor, adult learning and identifying community resources to support beginning school counselors. For details, see their Web site: *http://isca-in.org/development/mentor.html*. The mentor handbook is available at: *www.doe.state.in.us/dps/beginningteachers/manuals/school_counselor_mentor.pdf*.

A number of school systems are considering phased retirement programs, allowing senior employees to reduce their work hours over time as they move toward gradually disengaging from their positions. Retired school counselors are also a potential pool of mentors. Pre-retirement or retired school counselors usually want to ensure the continuation and success of the programs in which they invested time and effort during their years of employment. They are important sources of institutional history, political know-how and social support. Retired school counselors may be willing to volunteer to mentor new school counselors settling into the school system.

A quick Google search reveals a number of state school counselor associations, statewide departments of education, or school districts offering induction programs with mentoring for new school counselors. The Web sites listed below represents a sampling of this trend.

- *http://dese.mo.gov/divcareered/guide_mentoring.htm*
- *www.ncschoolcounselor.org/mentoring.asp*
- *www.scschoolcounselor.org/uploads/Resources/Mentoring_network.asp*
- *www2.edutech.nodak.edu/ndsca/mentoring.htm*
- *www.ilcounseling.org/displaycommon.cfm?an=1&subarticlenbr=39*

It is likely the design and evaluation of a mentor program will occur in stages, starting from an awareness of the importance of the program to finally institutionalizing it. The following table outlines rubrics for the various stages of mentoring program development.

Criteria for Designing and Evaluating a Mentor Program in School Counseling

PROFESSIONAL DEVELOPMENT AND TRAINING FOR MENTORS

Emerging Interest	Building Capacity	Deepening Practice	Sustaining Programs
No criteria exist for selecting mentors.	Mentors volunteer for the role.	Program administrators identify criteria for selecting mentors.	Program administrators identify criteria for selecting mentors.
Program administrators name mentors.	Program administrators hold an orientation session to outline mentors' roles and responsibilities.	Program administrators hold an orientation session for mentors and protégés to outline roles and responsibilities.	Program administrators hold an orientation session for mentors and protégés to outline roles and responsibilities.
			Mentors complete three days of training prior to the start of the school year. Program administrators attend the first day and protégés the last day.
Training consists of review of employee handbook with mentors.	Training includes qualities of effective mentors, needs of protégés, communication and questioning skills.	Training includes qualities of effective mentors, needs of protégés, communication, questioning skills and data-gathering techniques.	Training includes qualities of effective mentors, needs of protégés, communication, questioning skills and data-gathering techniques.
			Training provides opportunities to role play and practice mentoring skills.
		A follow-up session is held at mid-year.	Follow-up sessions are held monthly during the school year.
			Mentors and protégés review their work, including audio or video-based reflection.

Emerging Interest	Building Capacity	Deepening Practice	Sustaining Programs
Mentors express opinions about the program.	Evaluation focuses onparticipant satisfaction with orientation session.	Evaluation focuses on participant satisfaction with orientation session.	Evaluation focuses on participant satisfaction with orientation session.
		Program administrators conduct a survey of protégé needs to determine how well the mentor program addresses those needs.	Program administrators conduct a survey of protégé needs to determine how well the mentor program addresses those needs.
		Program administrators assess the impact of mentor training in supporting mentors to fulfill their roles.	Program administrators assess the impact of mentor training in supporting mentors to fulfill their roles.
		Program administrators use a rubric to define the criteria for determining the effectiveness of the program	Program administrators use a rubric to define the criteria for determining the effectiveness of the program
		Mentors self-assess their performance.	Mentors self-assess their performance.
		Program administrators analyze all data and use it to improve the program.	Program administrators analyze all data and use it to improve the program. Data-gathering and analysis include ways to determine the impact of the mentor program on protégés' practice of school counseling and ultimately, the impact on students.

The quality of school counseling in promoting student achievement is the bottom line in evaluating a mentoring program. Research is still lacking about the direct connection between mentoring professionals and student achievement. University-school district partnerships might be helpful in documenting the connection. The effectiveness of a mentor training program needs to be evaluated from the perspectives of both the mentors and protégés. First, protégés can help decide some of the content for mentor training by completing a needs assessment, e.g., what do protégés hope to gain from a mentorship? Mentors could complete the same assessment, then program administrators could compare the two. A survey of mentor program participants can ascertain consumer satisfaction with the training session. Did mentors and protégés acquire new understanding about their roles and responsibilities?

At regular intervals during the mentoring process, protégés should report how well mentors are meeting their needs. Specific mentoring needs the protégés have in terms of vocational support, protection, collegiality, career advancement and friendship can be listed and then rated on a Likert-type scale. For example:

MENTORING EFFECTIVENESS SURVEY

Rate your level of agreement with each statement as it pertains to your mentor.

	Strongly Agree		Neutral		Strongly Disagree
Vocational Support					
1. My mentor offers assistance to help me carry out my job responsibilities.	5	4	3	2	1
2. I often work on projects collaboratively with my mentor.	5	4	3	2	1
Protection					
3. My mentor uses his/her influence within the school to my benefit.	5	4	3	2	1
4. My mentor protects me from situations that could negatively affect my career goals.	5	4	3	2	1

	Strongly Agree		Neutral		Strongly Disagree

Collegiality

5. My mentor and I socialize during work hours (lunch, coffee breaks, etc.). — 5 4 3 2 1

6. My mentor and I socialize outside of school. — 5 4 3 2 1

Career Advancement

7. My mentor offers specific strategies to achieve my career goals. — 5 4 3 2 1

8. My mentor explains the political realities of working in the school. — 5 4 3 2 1

Friendship

9. I trust my mentor. — 5 4 3 2 1

10. My mentor supports and encourages me in my work. — 5 4 3 2 1

Multicultural Awareness

11. My mentor understands and addresses issues of cultural diversity — 5 4 3 2 1

12. My mentor collaborates to strive for obtaining social justice within the school — 5 4 3 2 1

Mentors need to monitor how the protégés' school counseling practices are changing, i.e., fuller implementation of the ASCA National Model. Finally, measures of the impact of protégés' work on student academic, personal, social and/or career learning might include the following:

- *Artifacts* - What evidence exists of transformed school counseling? What themes emerge?
- *Rituals* - What types of new events occur at the school?
- *Communication* - Examine patterns of communication and collaboration. How do school counselors, teachers, administrators and parents interact and work together?
- *Innovation* - How are new school counseling programs introduced and accepted?
- *Leadership* - Are counselors becoming school leaders? How do protégés see themselves?

EXERCISE:

If you were to receive an award as an exemplary mentor, how would that award be worded?

Research Agenda

There is some evidence that mentoring is helpful in improving student learning and in enhancing the performance and retention of teachers (American Association of State Colleges and Universities, 2006). However, considerably less evidence exists for school counselors, in part because there are fewer mentoring programs in that field. Answers to the following questions will help us further understand the mentoring process and outcomes:

- What are the components of effective school counselor mentor and protégé training programs?
- How does mentoring help promote job satisfaction and productivity among school counselors?
- What are the effects of mentoring on school counselors' skill acquisition?
- How does mentoring for school counselors improve the educational system(s)?
- How can mentoring be used as a vehicle for reform in school counseling?
- What are the institutional barriers for schools in implementing mentoring programs?

Conclusion

The field of school counseling has relied generally on individual practitioners assuming responsibility for their own professional development. Arguably the best method of induction and for continuing professional development is through dialogue and support from colleagues. School counseling needs to move away from a reliance on informal mentoring by non-counselor supervisors and toward formal mentoring programs with experienced school counselors as mentors. Because school counselors have a strong inclination to do what they have trained to do as helpers, selling a guidance department on the idea of a formal mentoring program should be relatively easy!

The new vision for school counseling has extended the role of school counselors into the arena of leadership. Item 13 of ASCA National Model (2003) states: The professional school counselor is a student advocate, leader, collaborator and a system change agent. The recommendation by Lazovsky and Shimoni (2007) that school counselors be trained for a mentoring role is opportune given the adoption of coaching and supervision. It is also consistent with other recommendations (e.g., Jackson et al., 2002). The time has come for the school counseling profession to take a stand and strive to turn the mentoring role into a high-status, prestigious professional role.

Case Studies

1: SUPPORTING INNOVATIVE IDEAS

You are mentoring a new school counselor who initiated and directs an after-school homework program at a community center. An outcomes-based program evaluation (conducted by the school counselor) indicated the program was successful in increasing homework completion rates. Parents and teachers are very pleased with the program and grateful to the school counselor for arranging it. Now, however, the school has a new principal who thinks this type of outreach is an inappropriate role for school counselors and wants the homework program to be taken over by the special education department. What can the mentor do to support innovative ideas? Are there ethical issues?

2: INFORMAL NETWORKS

You are mentoring a newly hired school counselor who is assigned to two different schools: an elementary and middle school. After several months, the school counselor discovered that the school psychologist in one building is the speech pathologist's sister in the second building, that the secretary at the elementary school is dating the principal of the middle school and that the director of pupil/personnel services is living with the director of special education. What is the mentor's role in advising the protégé of informal alliances and structures in the school system? What are the ethical issues?

3: PROFESSIONAL ATTIRE

Your protégé, the guidance department's most recently hired counselor, returned to work after winter break with a radically changed appearance and style of dress. She wore studded jeans, and she sported a pierced nose, lip and tongue. A few teachers and administrators requested to have her reassigned because of her "unprofessional" appearance. How should a mentor handle the matter of professional dress codes?

4: ROLE DEFINITION

Your protégé voiced complaints about having been asked by the school principal to cover classes when teachers are out ill and to perform menial tasks (i.e., filing, keeping track of attendance, answering the phone). How can a mentor help the protégé in this case?

5: PROFESSIONAL DEVELOPMENT

When initially hired, a school counselor was placed at a high school because he had indicated his strength was crisis intervention counseling. As you mentored him during his first year of employment, you observed his skill as a crisis counselor but noticed relatively weak skills in areas such as college advising, career counseling and consultation. During the past year, he has not made any progress in these areas, possibly because of the laissez-faire climate at the high school. Although he wants to remain at the high school, you feel an assignment at a different high school in the district would be beneficial for his professional growth. How can a mentor address this issue of professional development?

6: ENCOURAGING PROFESSIONAL INDEPENDENCE

Your protégé is eager and enthusiastic - and looks quite young. The majority of school staff members are nearing retirement. They have seen many educational fads come and go over the years and have little patience with a young, enthusiastic school counselor. The teachers in the school consistently turn to you instead of your protégé to handle matters well within your protégés capabilities and responsibilities. How can a mentor encourage professional independence under these circumstances?

7: ASSIGNING CREDIT FOR SUCCESSFUL PROJECTS

Your protégé comes to you with concerns about numerous discipline referrals and negative school climate issues, but has only a vague idea about how to address them. In your mentoring role, you suggest investigating and implementing a school-wide positive discipline program. You make suggestions for programs to explore, contact administrators to gain approval for the program, and help arrange implementation. The program is very successful in reducing discipline referrals and improving school climate. The school board wants to recognize the person(s) responsible for the program. How should credit be assigned?

8: RECOMMENDATIONS

Your protégé (who has been progressing nicely) asks you to recommend him for a school counselor director position within your school district. If he acquires the director position, your protégé would become your supervisor. Although you expect your protégé will be a leader one day, you do not feel he is ready to assume a director position. How would you handle the matter of a recommendation?

9: ADDRESSING DIVERSE PERSPECTIVES

Your protégé (who is African American) shares that she was invited to participate in the latest school staff retreat. In discussing her experience, she informs you that on several occasions she felt her contributions were not valued. You believe your protégé can offer a unique perspective to various issues and is a valuable asset to the school. How would you address your protégé's experiences?

For discussion among mentors

- Your protégé confides some personal problems. At first, you offer advice, but now personal issues seem to be the focus of your mentoring meetings. How can you steer the conversation back to professional-development issues?
- Your protégé spends too much time gossiping about others. What might be a strategy to redirect the conversation?
- Your protégé is struggling in the job role and is considering looking for a job in another school system. What would you do?

For discussion among protégés

- Your mentor is not returning your phone calls or e-mails. What should you do?
- Your mentor seems to be offering a lot advice about what to do, but not really listening to your concerns. What would you do?
- Your mentor seems distracted when you are talking and you're not sure (s)he heard everything you said. What should you do?

References

Agnew, T., Vaught, C.C., Getz, H.G., & Fortune, J. (2000). Peer group clinical supervision program fosters confidence and professionalism. *Professional School Counseling, 4*, 6-12.

Ambrose, L. (2003). Mentoring diversity: Serving a diverse patient population calls for diverse leadership. *Healthcare Executive*, September/October. Retrieved February 1, 2009, from *www.ache.org/newclub/CAREER/MentorArticles/Diversity.cfm*

American Association of State Colleges and Universities. (October, 2006). *Teacher induction programs: Trends and opportunities*. Washington, DC: Author. Retrieved September 17, 2008 from *www.aascu.org/policy_matters/pdf/v3n10.pdf*.

American School Counselor Association. (2004). *Ethical standards for school counselors*. Alexandria, VA: Author. Retrieved August 25, 2008 from *www.schoolcounselor.org/content.asp?contentid=173*.

American School Counselor Association. (2003). *The ASCA National Model: A framework for school counseling programs*. Alexandria, VA: Author.

Anderson, E.M., & Shannon, A.L. (1988). Toward a conceptualization of mentoring. *Journal of Teacher Education, 39*, 38-42.

Armstrong, S.A., Balkin, R.S., Long, R., & Caldwell, C. (2006). *Mentoring programs for first-year elementary school counselors: An exploratory study*. Retrieved September 17, 2007 from *www.jsc.montana.edu/articles/v4n19.pdf*.

Baker, S., Daniels, T., & Greely, A. (1990). Systematic training of graduate-level counselors: Narrative and meta-analytic reviews of three major programs. *Counseling Psychologist, 18*, 355-421.

Barker, M.J. (2007). Cross-cultural mentoring in institutional contexts. *The Negro Educational Review, 58*(1-2), 85-103.

Barlow, N. (Ed.). (1967). *Darwin and Henslow: The growth of an idea - letters 1831-1861*. Berkeley, CA: University of California Press.

Barnes, G., Crowe, E., & Schaefer, B. (2007). *The cost of teacher turnover in five school districts*. Retrieved September 17, 2008 from *www.nctaf.org/resources/demonstration_projects/turnover/documents/CTTExecutiveSummaryfinal.pdf*.

Bemak, F., & Chung, R.C. (2005). Advocacy as a critical role for urban school counselors: Working toward equity and social justice. *Professional School Counseling, 8*, 196-202.

Benishek, L.A, Bieschke, K.J., Park, J., & Slattery, S.M. (2004). A multicultural feminist model of mentoring. *Journal of Multicultural Counseling and Development, 32*, 428-442.

Bierema, L.L., & Merriam, S.B. (2002). E-mentoring: Using computer-mediated communication to enhance the mentoring process. *Innovative Higher Education, 26*, 211-227.

Boyd, J.D., & Walker, P.B. (1975). The school counselor, the cactus, and supervision. *School Counselor, 23*, 103-107.

Coomey, S.M., & Wilczenski, F.L. (2005). Implications of technology for social and emotional communication. *Journal of Applied School Psychology, 21*, 127-139.

Darwin, C. (Author), & Barlow, N. (Ed.). (1958). *The autobiography of Charles Darwin: 1809 - 1882*. New York: W.W. Norton.

Desmond, K.J., West, J.D., & Bubenzer, D. L. (2007). Enriching the profession of school counseling by mentoring novice school counselors without teaching experience. *Guidance & Counseling, 21*(3). Retrieved May 17, 2008 from Academic Search Premier Database.

DeVoss, J.A., & Andrews, M.F. (2006). *School counselors as educational leaders*. NY: Lahaska Press.

Eby, L.T., & Allen, T.D. (2002). Further investigation of protégés' negative mentoring experiences. *Group and Organization Management, 27*, 456-479.

Hansman, C.A. (2001, June). *Who plans? Who participates? Critically examining mentoring programs*. Paper presented at the Annual Meeting of the Adult Education Research Conference (42nd, Lansing, MI, June 1-3, 2001).

Harvard Business Essentials: Coaching and Mentoring. (2004). Boston, MA: Harvard Business School Publishing.

Holcomb-McCoy, C. (2007). *School counseling to close the achievement gap: A social justice framework for success*. Thousand Oaks, CA: Corwin Press.

Jackson, C.M., Snow, B.M., Boes, S.R., Phillips, P.L., Powell-Stanard, R., Painter, L.C., et al. (2002). Inducting the transformed school counselor into the profession. *Theory into Practice, 41*, 177-185.

Janas, M. (1996). Mentoring the mentor: A challenge for staff development. *Journal of Staff Development, 17*(4). Retrieved August 19, 2008 from *www.nsdc.org/library/publications/jsd/janas174.cfm*.

Johnson, W.B. (2002). The intentional mentor: Strategies and guidelines for the practice of mentoring. *Professional Psychology: Research and Practice, 33*, 88-96.

Johnson, W.B. (2007). *On being a mentor: A guide for higher education faculty*. Mahwah, NJ: Lawrence Erlbaum, Inc.

Johnson-Bailey, J. & Cervero, R.M. (2004). Mentoring in black and white: The intricacies of cross-cultural mentoring. *Mentoring and Tutoring, 12*(1), 9-21.

Kasprisin, C.A., Boyle-Single, P., Single, R.M., Ferrier, J.L., & Muller, C.B. (2008). Improved mentor satisfaction: Emphasizing protégé training for adult-age mentoring dyads. *Mentoring and Tutoring: Partnerships in Learning, 16*, 163-174.

Kaye, B., & Jordan-Evans, S. (2005). *Love 'em or lose 'em: Getting good people to stay.* San Francisco: Berrett-Koehler Publishers.

Lazovsky, R., & Shimoni, A. (2007). The on-site mentor of counseling interns: Perceptions of idea role and actual role performance. *Journal of Counseling and Development, 85*, 303-316.

Lee, C. (2005). *Multicultural issues in counseling.* Alexandria, VA: American Counseling Association.

Leonard, E.C., & Hilgert, R.L. (2004). *Supervision: Concepts and practices of management* (9th ed.). Mason, OH: Thomson South-Western.

Lund, J. (1990). Alone! *School Counselor, 37*, 204-209.

Massachusetts School Counselor Association. (2009, September). MASCA emerging leaders program enters third year. *Counselor's Notebook, 46*(1), 10.

Matthes, W.A. (1992). Induction of counselors to the profession. *School Counselor, 39*, 245-250.

McGreevy, A. (1990). Darwin and teacher: An analysis of the mentorship between Charles Darwin and Professor John Henslow. *Gifted Child Quarterly, 34*, 5-9.

Mentor. Definition retrieved July 11, 2008 from *www.merriam-webster.com/dictionary/mentor.*

Mentorship. Retrieved July 6, 2008 from *http://en.wikipedia.org/wiki/Mentoring.*

Myrick, R.D. (1993). *Developmental guidance and counseling: A practical approach* (2nd ed.). Minneapolis, MN: Educational Media Corp.

Owens, D., Pernice-Duca, F., & Thomas, D. (2009, February 10). Post-training needs of urban high school counselors: Implications for counselor training programs. *Journal of School Counseling, 7*(17). Retrieved August 6, 2009 from www.jsc.montana.edu/articles/v7n17.pdf.

Peace, S.D. (1995). Addressing school counselor induction issues: A developmental counselor mentor model. *Elementary School Guidance & Counseling, 29*, 177-190.

Peace, S.D., & Sprinthall, N.A. (1998). Training schools counselors to supervise beginning counselors: Theory, research, and practice. *Professional School Counseling, 1*, 2-8.

Roberts, A. (1999). The origins of the term mentor. *History of Education Society Bulletin, 64*, 313-329.

Schweibert, V.L. (2000). *Mentoring: Creating connected, empowered relationships.* Alexandria, VA: American Counseling Association.

Smith, P. (2000). *A marriage (not) made in heaven: School administrators, counselors, and mentoring.* In V.L. Schwiebert, Mentoring: Creating Connected, Empowered Relationships (127-151). Alexandria, VA: American Counseling Association.

Spooner, S.E., & Stone, S.C. (1977). Maintenance of specific counseling skills over time. *Journal of Counseling Psychology, 24,* 66-71.

Tentoni, S. (1995). The mentoring of counseling students: A concept in search of a paradigm. *Counselor Education and Supervision, 35,* 32-42.

Torrance, E.P. (1984). *Mentor relationships: How they aid creative achievement, endure, change, and die.* Buffalo, NY: Bearly Ltd.

University of Massachusetts Amherst. (2007). *Mellon mutual mentoring initiative.* Amherst, MA: Office of Faculty Development.

VanZandt, C.E., & Perry, N.S. (1992). Helping the rookie counselor: A mentoring project. *School Counselor, 39,* 158-163.

Walker, J.A. (2006). A reconceptualization of mentoring in counselor education: Using a relational model to promote mutuality and embrace differences. *Journal of Humanistic Counseling, Education and Development, 45,* 60-69.

Wilczenski, F.L. (1997). Marking the school psychology lifespan: Entry into and exit from the profession. *School Psychology Review, 26,* 502-514.

Wilczenski, F.L., & Coomey, S.M. (2007). *A practical guide to service learning: Strategies to foster positive development in schools.* New York: Springer.

Wilczenski, F.L., & Schumacher, R.A., (2008). Service learning integrated into urban school counselor preparation. *Journal of School Counseling, 6*(12). Available: *www.jsc.montana.edu/articles/v6n12.pdf.*

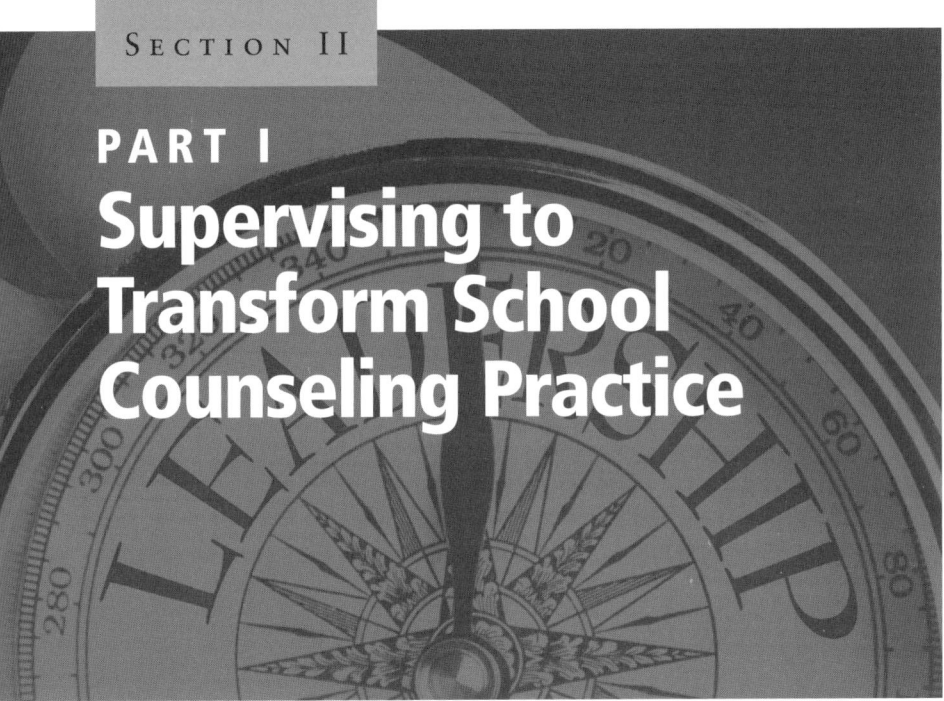

PART I
Supervising to Transform School Counseling Practice

*Children are the world's most valuable resource
and its best hope for the future ...*

JOHN F. KENNEDY (Kennedy, 1963)

Former President John F. Kennedy's vision for youth is as timely today as it was almost five decades ago. Irrespective of the decade, there is little denial that children and the education of children are of paramount influence in the future of our country.

Since the 1960s there has been a seismic change in education. Our 21st century schools and school issues are far different from those educators grappled with at the turn of the 20th century. Accountability for high-stakes testing, measuring educational achievement, standards-based reform, achievement gaps, learning needs and adequate yearly progress are current issues stemming from the educational reform movement and the federal *No Child Left Behind* (2001) legislation.

School counseling: highlights of reform

As our educational system has shifted to an accountability model, so has the profession of school counseling. Equality, equity, achievement, access to opportunities and success for all children are familiar phrases to school counselors. Educational reform and the age of educational accountability have significantly influenced the profession of school counseling.

REFLECTION: YOUR CAREER AS A PROFESSIONAL SCHOOL COUNSELOR

For readers who have been a professional school counselor for less than five years, think about when you were a k-12 student. What roles did your school counselor play in the school?

For those readers in the profession more than five years, how has your work changed since your first position as a school counselor?

Signs of altering conventional thinking about school counseling first emerged in the early 1990s in the work of Hart and Jacobi (1992). Their rallying cry encouraged school counselors to advocate for the success of all students (Hart & Jacobi). By the mid-1990s the Transforming School Counseling Initiative (Education Trust, 1997) spurred critical changes in school counseling. One significant change was the introduction of a "new vision" for school counseling, urging school counselors to shift from reactive service to a data-driven proactive program that could demonstrate outcomes and impact on k-12 students.

The second significant change reflected the "new vision" in higher education, where curricula for preparing school counselors saw dramatic changes (Education Trust). The American School Counselor Association's authorship of standards for school counseling programs (1998), followed by the development of the ASCA National Model (2003, 2005), further solidified how school counseling can operate in a much more proactive, programmed way in schools to demonstrate impact on k-12 students. The profession of school counseling entered the 21st century with a standardized, measureable plan, redefined roles and functions synthesized to serve all students equitably in academic, career and personal/social development (ASCA).

How we educate children in this country, as well as the profession of school counseling, have demonstrated recent dramatic changes. "As key partners in educational excellence, school counselors share the responsibility for educating all children" (Stone & Dahir, p. 19). School counseling can no longer be considered an ancillary service for some students, but rather a comprehensive, planned program for every k-12 student. Indeed, education for *all* children remains a critical issue. In a recent interview, U.S. Secretary of Education Arne Duncan commented:

> Achieving a quality education for all children is the civil rights issue of our generation. We have to give children a chance to fulfill their potential and be successful. And the way to do that is by giving them quality additional opportunities. That means that we have to reduce the dropout rate significantly. We have to increase the graduation rate. We have to make sure that the students who graduate are prepared to go on to be successful in some form of higher education, whether it's a two-year college, a four-year university, vocational, or technical training (Richardson, 2009, p. 24).

The issues Duncan raises – dropout/graduation rates and postsecondary planning – are fundamental concerns of a transformed school counseling program. There is evidence this paradigm shift to a transformed school counseling program has made, and can make a difference (Dahir & Stone, 2006). Having evidence is reassuring for the effort, but it neither discounts the challenge of the transformational process nor the mix of intrapersonal, interpersonal and systemic challenges generated within the process. Mentoring supports the efforts of delivering a transformed program.

The second principle for the 21st century, professional school counselor is the critical practice of supervision.

Supervision defined

Traditional thinking around supervision originated in the helping profession, most notably the mental-health field (Bernard & Goodyear, 2004). Cormier and Hackney (2008) suggested supervision can be distinctly categorized in different types, "clinical supervision and administrative supervision" (p. 183). To further clarify:

> Clinical supervision is an intervention that is provided by a senior member of a profession to a junior member or members of that same profession. This relationship is evaluative, extends over time, and has the simultaneous purposes of enhancing the professional functioning of the junior member(s), monitoring the quality of pro-

fessional services offered to the clients she, he, or they see(s), and serving as a gatekeeper for those who are to enter the particular profession (Bernard & Goodyear, 2004, p. 8).

Key themes in the definition indicate:

1. power differential between the two participants,
2. responsibility (to novice professional and clients),
3. professional development (advancement of knowledge and/or skills) and to a lesser degree,
4. informal evaluation.

An example of *conventional clinical supervision* would be a professional counselor, with 20 years experience, supervises a counselor in a community mental-health clinic. They meet weekly for one hour and discuss case conceptualization, interventions and issues of counseling presented by the counselor. The purpose is to enhance counseling for the client, and support professional development of the counselor. The senior counselor, counselor and clients seen by the counselor form a triad relationship.

The second type of supervision, *administrative supervision*, (Cormier and Hackney (2008, p. 183) is similar to clinical supervision with two exceptions: the organization is more the focus of supervision, and evaluation is emphasized. In administrative supervision, one individual of greater power and authority in an organization evaluates and oversees the performance of the member ranked lower in the organization. The focus of supervision is the interrelationship between the organization and member's contribution to the working of the organization.

Key themes in this definition indicate:

1. power differential between the two participants,
2. responsibility (to the professional of lesser power and the organization),
3. professional development (advancement of knowledge and/or skills), and
4. formal evaluation.

An example of *administrative supervision* would be an organization's director providing an annual, formal evaluation of the work of the organization's members. In addition, the director might meet periodically with members of the organization to support, guide or advise the work of members. A triad relationship exists between the director, member and organization.

Program supervision could be considered a subtype of administrative supervision because it contains some and/or similar characteristics of administrative supervision. Program supervision "involves a focus on program and includes program development, management and accountability" (Dollarhide & Miller, 2006, p. 244).

REFLECTION: SUPERVISION

How do you define supervision?
What type of supervision is prevalent in your school?

School counseling supervision

Historically, supervision for school counselors has been mostly limited to administrative supervision. Unlike administrative supervision in the mental-health field, supervision is often completed by an administrator who may or may not have a background in school counseling. During the 1970s, supervision was all but absent for school counselors, except for administrative supervision. Roger Aubrey (1973) speculated that building principals discouraged supervision to maintain their authority as supervisors, and also that counselor-education programs used a narrowly focused model of supervision not transferrable to schools. Boyd and Walter (1975) believed supervision was essential for school counselors and reasonably attainable. They proposed training counselors with the most experience and success to supervise. The also suggested that supervision of school counselors be done from a consultative, counseling, evaluative and professional development approach (Boyd & Walter).

As recent as 2006, the *Counselor Education and Supervision* journal devoted a special issue to clinical supervision in schools. In that issue, Dollarhide & Miller, (2006) reported results from a number of studies on school counseling supervision, finding that "between 21% and 37% of respondents did not see the need for, or expressed no desire for, supervision" (p. 300). This is an intriguing finding from two perspectives. Considering reform efforts were well underway by 2006, one might assume supervision was a sorely needed practice to help transition to the transformed model. On the other hand, this was a special issue devoted to clinical supervision, a practice that school counselors may have recognized as unresponsive to their needs for transformed school counseling. Currently administrative supervision remains the most commonly used supervision in schools.

Whether causal factors are external, internal or a combination of both, school counseling supervision has been primarily an administrative process, equated with evaluation of performance. A different model for school counselors seems an apparent need.

REFLECTION: YOUR EXPERIENCES

What experiences have you had with clinical supervision, administrative supervision or program supervision?

Clinical supervision

Clinical supervision is one of two types of conventional supervision. As discussed previously, the clinical approach is commonly used with licensed professional counselors and mental-health providers, and is likely a function of the weekly schedule.

The transformed school counselors would not find clinical supervision as great a necessity because the predominant focus of services is not on the individual student, but on a comprehensive program approach that reaches all students. Transformed school counseling programs use brief, solution-focused approaches to counsel students about normal developmental issues. The ASCA ethics describe counseling as focused on the academic and career development of students (ASCA, 2004). When crisis and critical emotional issues arise, referrals are made to mental health professionals; "School counselors do not provide therapy" (ASCA, 2003, p. 42). For readers interested in learning about the clinical supervisory process and development of clinical skills and counseling knowledge, Bernard & Goodyear (2004), Borders & Leddick, (1987), and Stoltenberg, McNeill, and Delworth (1998) may be essential reading.

For supervision of school counselors in training, Studer's book provides a comprehensive work (Studer, 2006). An additional resource is the June 2006 special issue of the *Counselor Education and Supervision*. This special issue, devoted to clinical supervision provides:

- a supervision model for school counselors in training (Wood & Rayle, 2006);
- a description of supervising school counseling students without teaching experience (Peterson & Deuschle, 2006);
- explains how to apply the discrimination model to school counseling (Luke & Bernard, 2006); and
- a rationale for clinical supervision in schools (Miller & Dollarhide, 2006).

Administrative supervision

All schools require job evaluation of faculty performance. Generally either school board policy and/or teacher unions dictate the evaluation instrument of faculty. Instructional staff (teachers) and supportive staff (school counselors) may have the exact or similar instrument for yearly evaluations. Evaluation instruments used can be as varied as there are districts in this country. With transformed school counseling using comprehensive, data-driven programs, logic follows that the instrument used for evaluation of the school counselor(s) needs to reflect the actual work of the counselors. Specific criteria need to define the performance of program and counselors.

The School Counseling Department, Duval County Public Schools in Jacksonville, Fla. provides one such example. The district-level supervisors of guidance developed competencies and corresponding indicators for their evaluation instrument (Appendix A). The building principal or assigned administrator first observes the school counselor (see Appendix B, Part A), then completes the instrument in advance of their meeting, or completes the instrument collaboratively during the supervision meeting. The evaluative assessment evaluates both the delivery of the counseling program and the professional characteristics of the school counselor.

Because administrative supervision has had a longstanding position in schools and will undoubtedly remain as a permanent activity, district-level school counseling administrators can use the evaluation process as a method to educate building administrators about transformed school counseling. This action would initiate dialogue about how counseling programs and school counselors can impact all students. In addition, use of an assessment instrument reflective of transformed school counseling would aid in solidifying the principal support for the school counseling program and the administrator/school counselor partnership.

REFLECTION: EVALUATION

How was the evaluation instrument at your school/district developed? How does the instrument reflect your work?

Next, the Supervision for the Transformed School Counseling Program proposes an approach to supervision from a transformed perspective.

Supervision for Transformed School Counseling Program

Some principles of clinical supervision and administrative supervision compare with school counseling supervision, while other aspects of conventional supervision may not be transferrable. What are the similarities and differences between traditional supervision and transformed school counseling? Similarities are presented first in Figure 1.

FIGURE 1: SIMILARITIES OF SUPERVISION

Helping Professions i.e. Mental Health (Clinical)	School Counseling
Evaluative	Evaluative
Power differential	Power differential
Responsibility to the profession	Responsibility to the profession
Professional development	Professional development
Consistent schedule	Consistent schedule

Figure 1 depicts how the four themes of supervision identified previously parallel supervision conducted in both mental health and school counseling. Therefore, school counseling is not throwing the baby out with the bath water. Yet, there are significant differences.

What are the differences in supervision? Succinctly, if supervision is a purposeful undertaking, generally with at least two (or more) professionals, certain assumptions about factors present in supervision can be inferred. Present in supervision are:

1. *a model* - framework for the act of supervising,
2. *subject* - "the object of attention" (Webster, 1998, p. 730),
3. *focus* - action or behaviors of helping, and
4. *participants* - individuals participating in supervision.

Overall, transformed school counseling is much more extensive in scope. Students, parents, administrators, teachers, co-workers and community can be considered as "clientele" of school counselors. The work site (a school and school district) is essentially a comprehensive system with a host of dynamics operating at any one time. A school counselor, therefore, is very different from a mental-health helper who works much more in isolation from colleagues, and who works one-to-one with individuals or with small groups.

Figure 2 presents each of these four dimensions, comparing mental-health type of supervision and school counseling supervision.

FIGURE 2: DIFFERENCES OF SUPERVISION

Helping Professions i.e. Mental Health (Clinical)	School Counseling
Models: approach to supervision based on psychotherapy or developmental models	**Model:** approach to supervision based on a "program" model
Subject: individual or group counseling with clients	**Subject:** ASCA National Model: *Foundation, Management, Delivery, Accountability*
Focus: case conceptualization, theoretical approaches, counseling skills and counseling techniques/interventions for individual clients	**Focus:** roles of advocate, leader, collaborator, system change agent (and functions of these roles), as well as the use of skills/techniques/interventions in delivery of program for all students
Participants: ■ Supervisor (experienced counselor) ■ Supervisee (less-experienced counselor)	**Participants:** ■ Supervisor may be a building administrator, district-level administrator, experienced counselor, peers, stakeholders ■ Supervisee: school counselor who may or may not have an accumulation of professional experience

Model and Subject of Supervision: Supervision provides the content for interaction and discussion. Any one of the elements of the ASCA National Model (*Foundation, Delivery System, Management System,* and/or *Accountability*) may be discussed during supervision.

Focus: Roles, functions and skills/interventions/strategies are the focus of supervision. Structure to the dialogue is essential; otherwise time spent may become no more than casual conversation. Processing can provide the necessary structure. Processing is a skill used by group workers to purposefully maximize learning from the group experience (DeLucia-Waack, 2006; Smead, 1995). "Engaging members in processing encourages them to learn about themselves and one another" (DeLucia-Waack, p. 158). Smead proposed that processing "involves questioning at four levels ... these four levels concern the intrapersonal dimension; the interpersonal dimension; new thoughts, feelings, or behaviors; and use or application of new knowledge" (p. 160). Processing in supervision would aid in discussing intrapersonal and interpersonal factors, as well as learning that occurs from use of a program.

FIGURE 3: SAMPLE QUESTIONS

Processing Dimensions	Sample Questions
Intrapersonal	What were you thinking when you reviewed the attendance data and found that so many students are absent on Mondays and rainy days?
Interpersonal	What did you learn from working with the math department?
Program Application	From the work completed thus far, what do you see as the next step for implementation of the tutoring program?

Participants: Contrary to supervision for other helping professions, school counseling is much more comprehensive in the roles and functions of a school counselor. Thus, the subject and focus as described above are significantly different, as well as participants are significantly different. Unlike traditional supervision that commonly has two participants, supervision in the context of school counseling is much broader. More people are involved in program delivery and consequently school counselors work with a multitude of people in a multitude of ways. Identified in Figure 4 are four, different possible supervisors that a school counselor may encounter.

FIGURE 4: PARTICIPANTS OF SUPERVISION

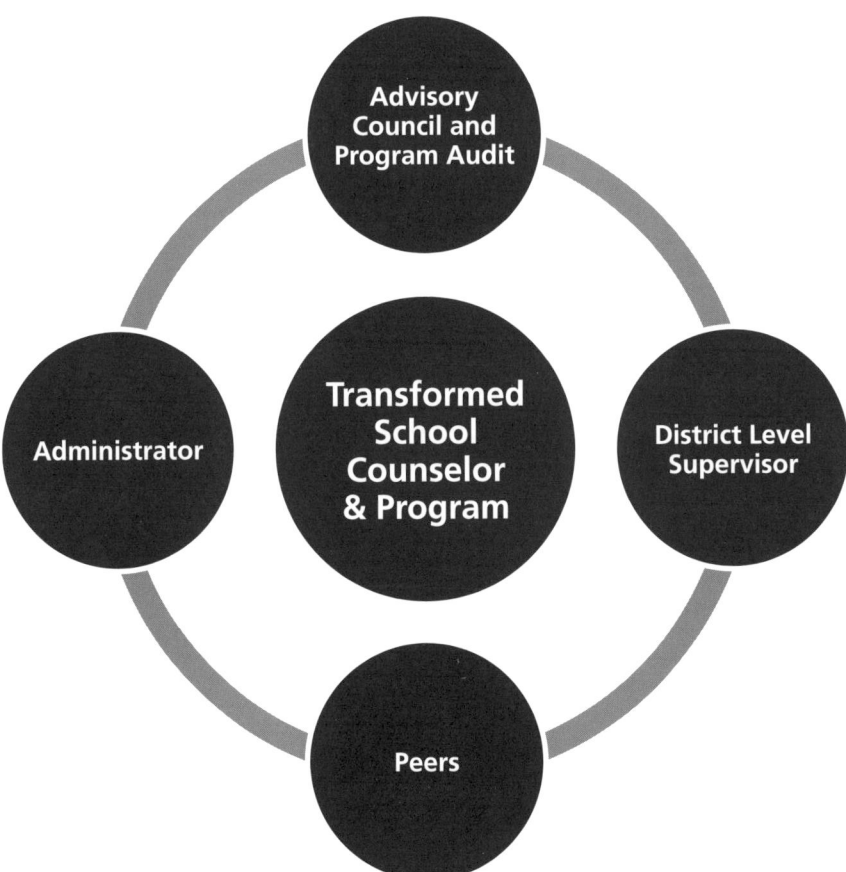

Administrators and district supervisors of school counseling programs are probably more commonly thought of as supervisory resources. Third participants (who can be extremely helpful) are peers. Fourth-level participants to consider are the program audit and the advisory council. The ASCA National Model (2005) suggests a component of a program have an advisory council of members representing the school and community. The function of the council is "to advise and assist the school counseling program within a school district" (p. 47). Additionally, the ASCA National Model calls for a Program Audit to provide an evaluation and modification tool:

- What components of the program are effective?
- What impact has the counseling program and work of the school counselor had on students?
- What do the results indicate for areas of needed improvement of medications?
- What does the school counselor need in professional development to implement changes in the program for increased effectiveness?

The combination of the work with the Advisory Council and completing the Program Audit provide:

1. outcomes (*an evaluation*) of specific criteria for the program, which are a reflection of the work of the school counselor(s);
2. shared power between members of the Council, the school counselor(s), and the program, rather than a *power differential;*
3. *responsibility* for the program and the impact the program has on students; and
4. resources that may be needed that very well may require *professional development.*

In a non-traditional sense, the Advisory Council and Program Audit serve as supervision for the school counselor and school counseling program.

Research

New paradigms generate the need for further study. Supervision and the transformed school counseling program raise many more questions than the body of research currently can answer. Both quantitative and qualitative findings would yield more insight into this needed practice in schools. Some possible areas for investigation are:

- What is the impact on students when the school counselor receives supervision?
- What is effective supervision in schools?
- How is effective supervision delivered?
- How does supervision impact the role, function and delivery of program?

- How does supervision influence a partnership of counselor, teacher and principal?
- What are the critical factors in the supervisory process?
- What are the similarities and differences for supervision for elementary-, middle- and secondary-level school counselors?

Conclusion

This chapter is designed to introduce supervision as one component of a transformed school counseling practice. It is just that; an introduction. Supervision for school counseling is an old concept in new clothing. For the advancement of the profession, it is critical the supervision be examined, refined and reshaped as a good fit for the 21st century, transformed school counselor. Supervision should be viewed not as "another task" to do, but as a means to an effective school counseling program that significantly impacts the success of every child in a school. For in the end, it is about *our most valuable resource, our children, and the hope for the future* (Kennedy, J., 1963).

References

American School Counselor Association. (2003). *The ASCA National Model: A framework for school counseling program.* Alexandria, VA: Author.

American School Counselor Association. (2004a). *Ethical standards for school counselors.* Retrieved September 12, 2009, from *www.schoolcounselor.org*.

American School Counselor Association. (2005). *The ASCA National Model: A framework for school counseling program* (2nd ed.). Alexandria, VA: Author.

Aubry, R. F. (1973). The organizational victimization of school counselors. *The School Counselor, 20,* 346-354.

Bernard, J.M. & Goodyear, R.K. (2004). *Fundamental of clinical supervision* (3rd ed.). Needham Heights, MA: Allyn & Bacon.

Borders, L.D. & Leddick, G.R. (1987). *Handbook of counseling supervision.* Alexandria, VA: Association for Counselor Education and Supervision.

Boyd, J.D. & Walter, P. B. (1975). The school counselor, the cactus, and supervision. *The School Counselor, 23,* 103-107.

Cormier, S. & Hackney, H. (2008). *Counseling strategies and interventions* (7th ed.). Boston, MA: Pearson.

Dahir, C., Sheldon, C.B. & Valiga, M.J. (1998). *Vision into action: Implementing the national standards for school counseling programs.* Alexandria, VA: American School Counselor Association.

Dahir, C. & Stone, C.B. (2006). *School counselor accountability: A measure of student success* (2nd ed.). Boston, MA: Pearson Merrill Prentice Hall.

DeLucia-Waack, J. L. (2006). *Leading psychoeducational groups for children and adolescents.* Thousand Oaks, CA: Sage Publications.

Dollarhide, C. T. & Miller, G. M. (2006). Special section: Supervision in schools. *Counselor Education and Supervision, 45,* 242-252.

Education Trust. (1997). *Working definition of school counseling.* Washington, DC: Author.

Hart, P. & Jacobi, M. (1992). *Gatekeeper to advocate.* New York: College Board Press.

Kennedy, J.F. (1963, July 25). UNICEF Appeal. Retrieved November 10, 2009 from *www.thekennedyway.com/quotes.htm*

Luke, M. & Bernard, J. M. (2006). The school counseling supervision model: An extension of the discrimination model. *Counselor Education and Supervision, 45,* 282-295.

Miller, G.M. & Dollarhide, C. T. (2006). Supervision in schools: Building pathways to excellence. *Counselor Education and Supervision, 45,* 296-303.

Peterson, J. S. & Deuschle, C. (2006). A model for supervising school counseling students without teaching experience. *Counselor Education and Supervision, 45,* 267-281.

No Child Left Behind Act of 2001, Pub. L. 107-110, No. 115, Stat. 1425 (2001).

Richardson, J. (2009). Quality education is our moon shot. *Phi Delta Kappan, 91*(1), 24-29.

Smead, R. (1995). *Skills and techniques for group work with children and adolescents.* Champaign, IL: Research Press.

Stoltenberg, C.D., McNeill, B.& Delworth, U. (1998). *IDM supervision: An integrated developmental model for supervising counselors and therapists.* San Francisco: Jossey-Bass.

Stone, C.B. & Dahir, C. (2006). *The transformed school counselor.* Boston, MA: Lahaska Press.

Studer, J. R. (2006). *Supervising the school counselor trainee: Guidelines for practice.* Alexandria, VA: American Counseling Association.

"Supervision in Schools." (2006). [Special Issue]. *Counselor Education and Supervision, 45,* 242-303.

Webster, M. (1998). *Collegiate Dictionary.* (11th ed.). Springfield, MA: Author.

Wood, C. & Rayle, A.D. (2006). A model of school counseling supervision: The goals, functions, roles, and systems model. *Counselor Education and Supervision, 45,* 253-266.

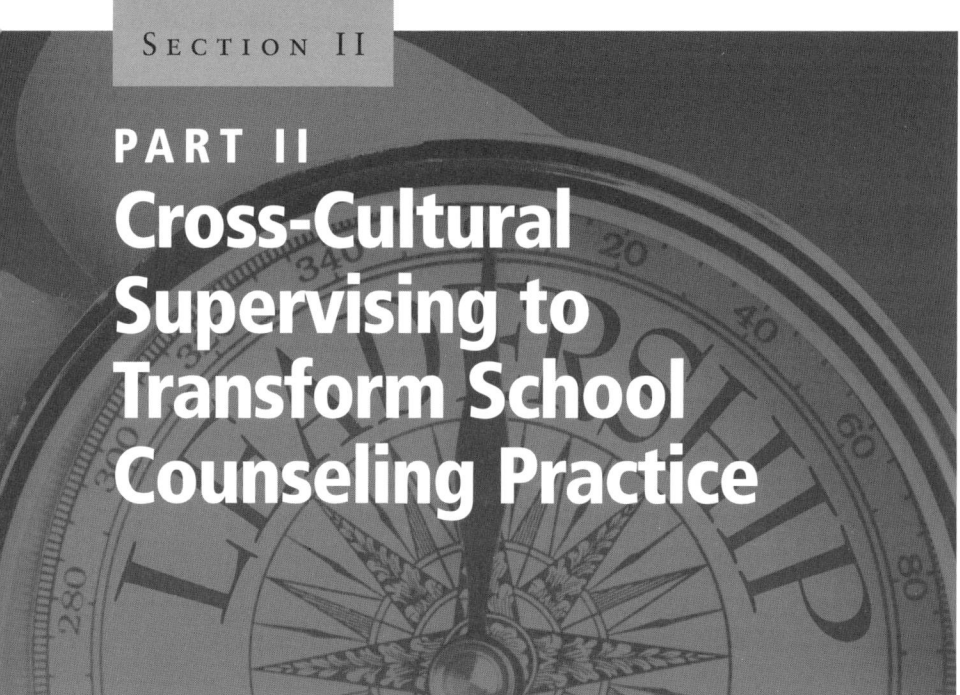

SECTION II

PART II
Cross-Cultural Supervising to Transform School Counseling Practice

Numerous researchers have identified the need for cross-cultural or multi-cultural supervision training (Estrada, Frame, & Williams, 2004; Toporek, Ortega-Villalobos, Pope-Davis, 2004; Hird, Cavalieri, Dulko, Felice, & Ho, 2001; Daniels, D'Andrea, & Kim, 1999). However, the majority of supervisors do not receive such training despite the fact that counselor education graduate programs typically emphasize the importance of developing cultural competency. As a result, this discrepancy can create tension during supervision when supervisees perceive supervisors to display limited sensitivity to issues regarding diversity (Burkard, Johnson, Madson, Pruitt, Contreras-Tadych, Kozlowski, Hess, & Knox, 2006).

Cross-cultural supervision (also commonly referred to as multicultural supervision) includes the discussion of ethnicity, race, gender, socioeconomic status, sexual orientation, disability status and religion or spirituality (Estrada et al., 2004). Given the significant increase in diverse student and family populations served by school counselors in the United States, it is imperative that supervisors provide supervision inclusive of all cultural backgrounds, regardless of difference in cultural background between the supervisor and supervisee. Failure to acknowledge and discuss the impact of culture in supervision risks perpetuating the status quo of ignoring relevant cultural issues important to students, parents (caretakers) and supervisees. Relying on traditional supervisory models that reflect the dominant ethnocentric ideology tends to endorse values and belief systems of the majority population (Daniels et al., 1999).

Garrett, Borders, Crutchfield, Torres-Rivera, Brotherton, & Curtis (2001) found significant support in the literature identifying the need for supervisors to examine their own assumptions, beliefs and awareness with regard to cultural differences. Inability to do so precludes supervisors from facilitating supervisees' growth and awareness with respect to multicultural issues and working effectively on behalf of students. In addition, Garrett and colleagues emphasize the importance of addressing the possible presence of power differentials and cultural differences between the supervisor and supervisee. Thus, it is not sufficient for the supervisor to address solely the power and cultural differences between the supervisee and students on the supervisee's case load. Handling power differentials and differences in cultural awareness are also relevant when the supervisor and supervisee are peers and engage in peer supervision. This is because there may be perceived differences in status, experience or position within the school. Supervisors must also initiate the discussion of multicultural issues in the supervisory relationship when they are in an evaluative position (Garrett et al.). As such, it is imperative that supervisors feel comfortable with their own self-identity and cultural awareness.

Addressing diversity issues helps supervisees (and supervisors) acquire greater knowledge in conceptualizing student needs and improves their ability to work with students and parents and/or caretakers from diverse backgrounds. Through conducting a qualitative research study examining 13 supervisees' experiences of supervision, Burkard and colleagues (2006) discovered the working relationship between supervisor and supervisee grew stronger when the supervisor and supervisee discussed the presence of cultural differences in the dyad. More specifically, the supervisees reported feeling safer, more comfortable and were overall more satisfied with the supervisory experience.

Suggestions for implementing multicultural supervision

Researchers have provided many suggestions for implementing effective multicultural or cross-cultural supervision. Discussion of multicultural issues in the supervisory relationship should take place early, to dispel misguided beliefs or assumptions about the supervisor and supervisee (Hird et al., 2001; Daniels et al., 1999). This discussion should focus on talking about how multicultural issues influence the supervisee's (and supervisor's) lives (Estrada et al., 2004). In doing so, the supervisor can assess the supervisee's level of racial awareness, cultural awareness and comfort level.

Communication is also instrumental in fostering a successful supervisory relationship (Garrett et al., 2001). Different communication styles can take place in supervisory dyads (including peer-supervisory dyads), particularly when the supervisor and supervisee hold different values and come from different cultural backgrounds. It is essential for the supervisor to process cultural differences both within the supervisory relationship and the counseling relationships the supervisee encounters. Hird and colleagues (2001) also encourage the use of self-disclosure regarding the supervisor's vulnerabilities in handling cultural diversity issues to facilitate the supervisee's development of multicultural awareness and skills. In addition, self-disclosure of this nature helps balance the power differential inherent in most supervisory relationships, including peer supervisory relationships.

Estrada and colleagues (2004) identified the following three strategies to cultivate effective multicultural supervision:

1. Create an environment of trust in which the supervisee feels safe to share fears and mistakes.
2. The supervisor and supervisee need to assess their own awareness of racial and ethnic backgrounds and how their personal beliefs regarding culture could potentially influence the supervisory relationship. It can be helpful if they complete cultural genograms to explore cultural background, belief systems and any feelings of shame or discomfort. In addition, they can use racial-identity inventories to measure awareness level and cultural sensitivity (such as the Black Racial Identity Attitude Scale and the White Racial Identity Attitude Scale). They could then discuss the results of the inventories in supervision.
3. Encourage supervisees to learn about their students' cultural backgrounds through reading relevant literature and engaging in the students' community. Encourage the supervisor to do the same.

Other researchers have offered suggestions for implementing multicultural supervision. Daniels and colleagues (1999) identified the importance of engaging in the following activities:

1. Initiate discussion regarding supervisor's and supervisee's cultural background.
2. Explore how one's values and philosophical perspective associated with one's cultural background influence counseling goals and supervisory expectations.
3. Discuss strengths and limitations or knowledge and lack of knowledge regarding multicultural counseling and supervision.
4. Increase awareness of and familiarity with racial identity models.
5. Engage in discussion of how supervisor's and supervisee's level of racial identity awareness could potentially impact one's counseling and supervisory perspective.
6. Express interest in learning about supervisee's cultural perspectives and beliefs.

Garrett and colleagues (2001) suggest using the acronym VISION in addressing issues of multiculturalism in the supervisory relationship:

V alues or belief system of the supervisee

I nterpretation of the supervisee's worldview, including his or her experience of supervision

S tructure of the supervisee's worldview according to cultural meanings and preferences and how the supervision is structured (content versus process of supervision)

I nteraction style or preferred communication style

O perational strategies that are used with regard to accomplishing counseling and supervisory goals. How are goals selected and worked toward in accordance with a particular perspective or cultural preference?

N eeds, including physical, mental, spiritual, and environmental. What are the supervisor's goals and the supervisee's needs?

Models of multicultural supervision

In reviewing the counselor-educator literature, Lassiter, Napolitano, Culbreth, & Ng (2008) identified numerous models of supervision, including psychodynamic models and developmental models. For example, Studer (2006) identified four developmental stages supervisees should move through, provided the supervisor effectively supports the supervisee. Stage one (orientation) is characterized as the learning phase. During this stage, it is critical supervisors set the tone and direction of the supervision to come. The next stage (transformation) occurs during the middle stages of supervision. During this stage, significant growth is expected in terms of developing counseling skills and autonomy. However, the supervisee still experiences anxiety when faced with new situations. During the third stage (professional direction) supervisees have integrated those counseling skills they are comfortable with to form a foundation for further growth. The final stage (integration) occurs when the supervisee has reached full autonomy and uses support of colleagues in a collaborative manner. This and other supervision models are typically applied to providing multicultural supervision but alone may not be sufficient in addressing gender and cross-cultural issues within the supervisory relationship. Some of the more recent models of supervision better address multiculturalism.

Ober, Granello, & Henfield (2009) introduced a model of multicultural supervision called the Synergistic Model of Multicultural Supervision (SMMS). The SMMS incorporates both developmental aspects and multicultural components to the supervisory process. It recognizes the notion that supervisors and supervisees move through stages within the supervisory relationship while concomitantly incorporating the multiplicity of self-identities that may be present. In addition, the model focuses on facilitating the development of multicultural competencies in counseling relationships outside of the supervisory dyad.

Feminist-multicultural supervision focuses on empowering supervisees within the supervisory relationship given the inherent power difference present (Nelson, Gizara, Hope, Phelps, Steward, & Weitzman, 2006). With such a focus, it is the responsibility of the supervisor to engage in discussions of gender and cross-cultural differences that may exist within the supervisory relationship. Nelson and colleagues identify the possibility for such discussion to engender feelings of discomfort and even distancing, particularly when the supervisee (and supervisor) is (are) not ready to address such issues. In addition, a novice supervisor may feel apprehensive in addressing multicultural issues due to the need to feel appreciated and liked by the supervisee. Because of the potential for strong feelings to arise in addressing gender and cross-cultural issues, Nelson and colleagues (2006) emphasize the importance of receiving specific supervision training that addresses multicultural aspects within the supervisory relationship.

The feminist-multicultural model of supervision encourages the supervisor to discuss openly any practices of supervision that tend to engender inequality in the supervisory relationship. For example, the use of video- and audio-taping to assess supervisees' counseling skills is essential to ensure proper skill development and to monitor the supervisee's progress.

Yet this practice also emphasizes the evaluative nature and power differential of the supervisory relationship. Thus, in using video- and audio-taping methods of evaluation, it is important the supervisor is transparent, openly discussing the effects of such practices on the supervisory relationship (Nelson et al., 2006).

The Structured Peer Group Supervision (SPGS) Model has been applied to developing multicultural competence (Lassiter et al., 2008). The SPGS Model includes video- or audio-taping of a counseling session and presenting the content and process questions to the group. In doing so, each group member is given a specific role, such as the counselor or student, and is required to provide feedback accordingly. Lassiter and colleagues (2008) incorporated multicultural competencies to the SPGS Model through recommending the inclusion of identifying and discussing issues of diversity that are relevant in the recording. A group member is assigned a multicultural role, paying particular attention to power dynamics and issues regarding gender, race, ethnicity, disability, sexual orientation, etc. The facilitator encourages the responder to consider the counselor, student, or parent's (caretaker's) perspective vis-à-vis relevant diversity issues. The use of a multicultural framework with SPGS helps facilitate the development of multicultural competency for all participants.

Case Study
Addressing Diversity in Peer Supervision

You are engaging in peer supervision with a less-experienced school counselor and identify the need to discuss the cultural differences between you and your colleague. In doing so, you are concerned because your colleague took offense to the relevance you placed on the discussion. You wonder whether your colleague is comfortable with his racial identity. What steps would you take to address your colleague's reaction?

MULTICULTURAL SUPERVISION INVENTORY

Rate your level of agreement with each statement.

	Strongly Agree		Neutral		Strongly Disagree
Assumptions and Beliefs					
1. I am aware of my self-identity with respect to my cultural background and values.	5	4	3	2	1

2. I am aware of my limitations and strengths and how they influence the supervisory relationship.   5   4   3   2   1

3. I feel comfortable when interacting with individuals who may come from different cultural backgrounds.   5   4   3   2   1

4. I am aware of my biases and and beliefs in terms of race, ethnicity and culture and how they may impact the supervisory relationship.   5   4   3   2   1

5. I recognize power differentials that occur in supervisory relationships.   5   4   3   2   1

Knowledge and Skills

1. I have specific knowledge regarding my cultural background and how it impacts supervisory relationships.   5   4   3   2   1

2. I understand sociopolitical factors and how they influence an individual based on racial and cultural background.   5   4   3   2   1

3. I possess knowledge about life experiences, world views and historical perspectives of individuals from diverse cultural backgrounds.   5   4   3   2   1

4. I regularly seek opportunities to update my knowledge of supervisory skills, particularly in providing multicultural supervision.   5   4   3   2   1

5. I feel comfortable acknowledging and discussing cultural differences that may be present in the supervisory relationship.   5   4   3   2   1

6. I am aware of my communication style and make modifications as necessary.   5   4   3   2   1

References

Burkard, A. W., Johnson, A.J., Madson, M.B., Pruitt, N.T., Contreras-Tadych, D.A., Kozlowski, J.M., Hess, S.A., & Knox, S. (2006). Supervisor cultural responsiveness and unresponsiveness in cross-cultural supervision. *Journal of Counseling Psychology, 53*(3): 288-301.

Daniels, J., D'Andrea, M., & Kim, B.S.K. (1999). Assessing the barriers and changes of cross-cultural supervision: A case study. *Counselor Education and Supervision, 38*(3): 191-204.

Estrada, D., Frame, M.W., & Williams, C.B. (2004). Cross-cultural supervision: Guiding the conversation toward race and ethnicity. *Journal of Multicultural Counseling and Development, 32*, 307-319.

Garrett, M.T., Borders, L.D., Crutchfield, L.B., Torres-Rivera, E., Brotherton, D., & Curtis, R. (2001). Multicultural superVISION: A paradigm of cultural responsiveness for supervisors. *Journal of Multicultural Counseling and Development, 29*, 147-158.

Hird, J.S., Cavalieri, C.E., Dulko, J.P., Felice, A.A.D., & Ho, T.A. (2001). Visions and realities: Supervisee perspectives of multicultural supervision. *Journal of Multicultural Counseling and Development, 29*, 114-130.

Lassiter, P.S., Napolitano, L., Culbreth, J.R., & Ng, K. (2008). Developing multicultural competence using the structured peer group supervision model. *Counselor Education and Supervision, 47*, 164-178.

Nelson, M.L., Gizara, S., Hope, A.C., Phelps, R., Steward, R., & Weitzman, L. (2006). A feminist multicultural perspective on supervision. *Journal of Multicultural Counseling and Development, 34*, 105-115.

Ober, A.M., Granello, D.H., & Henfield, M.S. (2009). A synergistic model to enhance multicultural competence in supervision. *Counselor Education and Supervision, 48*, 204-221.

Studer, J.R. (2006). *Supervising the school counselor trainee: Guidelines for practice.* Alexandria, VA: American Counseling Association.

Toporek, R.L., Ortega-Villalobos, L., Pope-Davis, D.B. (2004). Critical incidents in multicultural supervision: Exploring supervisees' and supervisors' experiences. *Journal of Multicultural Counseling and Development, 32*, 66-83.

Conclusion

Leadership skills of mentoring and supervising are needed to meet the challenges of transformed roles for 21st century school counselors prescribed by the ASCA National Model. The ASCA National Model was designed by and for school counselors. The transformation can only occur if school counselors themselves take the lead to move the field forward. It is up to school counselors to acquire leadership expertise in mentoring and supervising to take advantage of resources available in their schools, support the professional development of colleagues at all career stages and ensure that school counseling remains integral to the academic mission of schools. We hope this book helps school counselors advance those goals.

Appendix A: School Counselor Competencies and Indicators

School Counselor Competencies

HISTORY AND PURPOSE

The American School Counselor Association (ASCA) supports school counselors' efforts to help students focus on academic, personal/social and career development so they achieve success in school and are prepared to lead fulfilling lives as responsible members of society. In recent years, the ASCA leadership has recognized the need for a more unified vision of the school counseling profession. "The ASCA National Model: A Framework for School Counseling Programs"was a landmark document that provided a mechanism with which school counselors and school counseling teams could design, coordinate, implement, manage and enhance their programs for students' success. The ASCA National Model® provides a framework for the program components, the school counselor's role in implementation and the underlying philosophies of leadership, advocacy, collaboration and systemic change.

The School Counselor Competencies continue the effort for a unified vision by outlining the knowledge, attitudes and skills that ensure school counselors are equipped to meet the rigorous demands of our profession and the needs of our Pre-K-12 students. These competencies are necessary to better ensure that our future school counselor workforce will be able to continue to make a positive difference in the lives of students.

DEVELOPMENT OF THE COMPETENCIES

The development of the School Counselor Competencies document was a highly collaborative effort among many members of the school counseling profession.

A group of school counseling professionals that included practicing school counselors, district school counseling supervisors and counselor educators from across the country met in January 2007 to discuss ways to ensure that school counselor education programs adequately train and prepare future school counselors to design and implement comprehensive school counseling programs. The group agreed that the logical first task should be the development of a set of competencies necessary and sufficient to be an effective professional school counselor.

The group created a general outline of competencies and asked ASCA to form a task force to develop draft school counselor competencies supporting the ASCA National Model. The task force used sample competencies from states, universities and other organizations to develop a first draft, which was presented to the whole group for feedback. After comments and revisions were incorporated, the revised draft was released for public review and comment. Revisions through the public comment were incorporated to develop the final version. The school counselor competencies document is unique in several ways. First, this set of competencies is organized around and consistent with the ASCA National Model. Second, the competencies are comprehensive in that they include skills, knowledge and attitudes necessary for meritoriously performing the range of school counselor responsibilities (e.g., counseling, coordinating, consulting, etc.) in all four components of comprehensive school counseling programs: foundation, management, delivery and accountability. These competencies have been identified as those that will equip new and experienced school counselors with the skills to establish, maintain and enhance a comprehensive, developmental, results-based school counseling program addressing academic achievement, personal and social development and career planning.

APPLICATIONS

ASCA views these competencies as being applicable along a continuum of areas. For instance, school counselor education programs may use the competencies as benchmarks for ensuring students graduate with the knowledge, skills and dispositions needed for developing comprehensive school counseling programs. Professional school counselors could use the School Counselor Competencies as a checklist to self-evaluate their own competencies and, as a result, formulate an appropriate professional development plan. School administrators may find these competencies useful as a guide for seeking and hiring highly competent school counselors and for developing meaningful school counselor performance evaluations. Also, the School Counselor Competencies include the necessary technological competencies needed for performing effectively and efficiently in the 21st century.

I. SCHOOL COUNSELING PROGRAMS

School counselors should possess the knowledge, abilities, skills and attitudes necessary to plan, organize, implement and evaluate a comprehensive, developmental, results-based school counseling program that aligns with the ASCA National Model.

I-A: Knowledge

ASCA's position statement, The Professional School Counselor and School Counseling Preparation Programs, states that school counselors should articulate and demonstrate an understanding of:

I-A-1   The organizational structure and governance of the American educational system as well as cultural, political and social influences on current educational practices

I-A-2.   The organizational structure and qualities of an effective school counseling program that aligns with the ASCA National Model

I-A-3.   Impediments to student learning and use of advocacy and data-driven school counseling practices to act effectively in closing the achievement/opportunity gap I-A-4. Leadership principles and theories

I-A-5.   Individual counseling, group counseling and classroom guidance programs ensuring equitable access to resources that promote academic achievement; personal, social and emotional development; and career development including the identification of appropriate post-secondary education for every student

I-A-6.   Collaborations with stakeholders such as parents and guardians, teachers, administrators and community leaders to create learning environments that promote educational equity and success for every student

I-A-7.   Legal, ethical and professional issues in pre-K—12 schools

I-A-8.   Developmental theory, learning theories, social justice theory, multiculturalism, counseling theories and career counseling theories

I-A-9.   The continuum of mental health services, including prevention and intervention strategies to enhance student success

I-B: Abilities and Skills

An effective school counselor is able to accomplish measurable objectives demonstrating the following abilities and skills.

I-B-1.   Plans, organizes, implements and evaluates a school counseling program aligning with the ASCA National Model

I-B-1a.   Creates a vision statement examining the professional and personal competencies and qualities a school counselor should possess

I-B-1b.   Describes the rationale for a comprehensive school counseling program

I-B-1c.   Articulates the school counseling themes of advocacy, leadership, collaboration and systemic change, which are critical to a successful school counseling program.

I-B-1d.   Describes, defines and identifies the qualities of an effective school counseling program

I-B-1e.   Describes the benefits of a comprehensive school counseling program for all stakeholders, including students, parents, teachers, administrators, school boards, department of education, school counselors, counselor educators, community stakeholders and business leaders

I-B-1f.   Describes the history of school counseling to create a context for the current state of the profession and comprehensive school counseling programs

I-B-1g.   Uses technology effectively and efficiently to plan, organize, implement and evaluate the comprehensive school counseling program

I-B-1h.   Demonstrates multicultural, ethical and professional competencies in planning, organizing, implementing and evaluating the comprehensive school counseling program

I-B-2.   Serves as a leader in the school and community to promote and support student success

I-B-2a.   Understands and defines leadership and its role in comprehensive school counseling programs

I-B-2b.   Identifies and applies a model of leadership to a comprehensive school counseling program

I-B-2c.   Identifies and demonstrates professional and personal qualities and skills of effective leaders

I-B-2d.   Identifies and applies components of the ASCA National Model requiring leadership, such as an advisory council, management system and accountability

I-B-2e.   Creates a plan to challenge the non-counseling tasks that are assigned to school counselors

I-B-3.   Advocates for student success

I-B-3a.   Understands and defines advocacy and its role in comprehensive school counseling programs

I-B-3b.   Identifies and demonstrates benefits of advocacy with school and community stakeholders

I-B-3c.   Describes school counselor advocacy competencies, which include dispositions, knowledge and skills

I-B-3d.   Reviews advocacy models and develops a personal advocacy plan

I-B-3e.   Understands the process for development of policy and procedures at the building, district, state and national levels

I-B-4.   Collaborates with parents, teachers, administrators, community leaders and other stakeholders to promote and support student success

I-B-4a.   Defines collaboration and its role in comprehensive school counseling programs

I-B-4b.   Identifies and applies models of collaboration for effective use in a school counseling program and understands the similarities and differences between consultation, collaboration and counseling and coordination strategies.

I-B-4c.   Creates statements or other documents delineating the various roles of student service providers, such as school social worker, school psychologist, school nurse, and identifies best practices for collaborating to affect student success

I-B-4d.   Understands and knows how to apply a consensus-building process to foster agreement in a group

I-B-4e.   Understands how to facilitate group meetings to effectively and efficiently meet group goals

I-B-5.   Acts as a systems change agent to create an environment promoting and supporting student success

I-B-5a.   Defines and understands system change and its role in comprehensive school counseling programs

I-B-5b.   Develops a plan to deal with personal (emotional and cognitive) and institutional resistance impeding the change process

I-B-5c.   Understands the impact of school, district and state educational policies, procedures and practices supporting and/or impeding student success

I-C: Attitudes
School counselors believe:

I-C-1. Every student can learn, and every student can succeed

I-C-2. Every student should have access to and opportunity for a high-quality education

1-C-3. Every student should graduate from high school and be prepared for employment or college and other postsecondary education

I-C-4. Every student should have access to a school counseling program

I-C-5. Effective school counseling is a collaborative process involving school counselors, students, parents, teachers, administrators, community leaders and other stakeholders

I-C-6. School counselors can and should be leaders in the school and district

I-C-7. The effectivness of school counseling programs should be measurable using process, perception and results data

II: FOUNDATIONS

School counselors should possess the knowledge, abilities, skills and attitudes necessary to establish the foundations of a school counseling program aligning with the ASCA National Model.

II-A: Knowledge
School counselors should articulate and demonstrate an understanding of:

II-A-1 Beliefs and philosophy of the school counseling program that align with current school improvement and student success initiatives at the school, district and state level

II-A-2 Educational systems, philosophies and theories and current trends in education, including federal and state legislation

II-A-3 Learning theories

II-A-4 History and purpose of school counseling, including traditional and transformed roles of school counselors

II-A-5 Human development theories and developmental issues affecting student success

II-A-6 District, state and national student standards and competencies, including ASCA Student Competencies

II-A-7 Legal and ethical standards and principles of the school counseling profession and educational systems, including district and building policies

II-A-8   Three domains of academic achievement, career planning, and personal and social development

II-B: Abilities and Skills

An effective school counselor is able to accomplish measurable objectives demonstrating the following abilities and skills.

II-B-1.   Develops the beliefs and philosophy of the school counseling program that align with current school improvement and student success initiatives at the school, district and state level

II-B-1a.   Examines personal, district and state beliefs, assumptions and philosophies about student success, specifically what they should know and be able to do

II-B-1b.   Demonstrates knowledge of a school's particular educational philosophy and mission

II-B-1c.   Conceptualizes and writes a personal philosophy about students, families, teachers, school counseling programs and the educational process consistent with the school's educational philosophy and mission

II-B-2.   Develops a school counseling mission statement aligning with the school, district and state mission.

II-B-2a.   Critiques a school district mission statement and identifies or writes a mission statement aligning with beliefs II-B-2b.Writes a school counseling mission statement that is specific, concise, clear and comprehensive, describing a school counseling program's purpose and a vision of the program's benefits every student

II-B-2c.   Communicates the philosophy and mission of the school counseling program to all appropriate stakeholders

II-B-3.   Uses student standards, such as ASCA Student Competencies, and district or state standards, to drive the implementation of a comprehensive school counseling program

II-B-3a.   Crosswalks the ASCA Student Competencies with other appropriate standards

II-B-3b.   Prioritizes student standards that align with the school's goals

II-B-4.   Applies the ethical standards and principles of the school counseling profession and adheres to the legal aspects of the role of the school counselor

II-B-4a.   Practices ethical principles of the school counseling profession in accordance with the ASCA Ethical Standards for School Counselors

II-B-4b.   Understands the legal and ethical nature of working in a pluralistic, multicultural, and technological society.

II-B-4c. Understands and practices in accordance with school district policy and local, state and federal statutory requirements.

II-B-4d. Understands the unique legal and ethical nature of working with minor students in a school setting.

II-B-4e. Advocates responsibly for school board policy, local, state and federal statutory requirements that are in the best interests of students

II-B-4f. Resolves ethical dilemmas by employing an ethical decision-making model appropriate to work in schools.

II-B-4g. Models ethical behavior II-B-4h. Continuously engages in professional development and uses resources to inform and guide ethical and legal work

II-B-4i. Practices within the ethical and statutory limits of confidentiality

II-B-4j. Continually seeks consultation and supervision to guide legal and ethical decision making and to recognize and resolve ethical dilemmas

II-B-4k. Understands and applies an ethical and legal obligation not only to students but to parents, administration and teachers as well

II-C: Attitudes

School counselors believe:

II-C-1. School counseling is an organized program for every student and not a series of services provided only to students in need

II-C-2. School counseling programs should be an integral component of student success and the overall mission of schools and school districts

II-C-3. School counseling programs promote and support academic achievement, personal and social development and career planning for every student

II-C-4. School counselors operate within a framework of school and district policies, state laws and regulations and professional ethics standards

III: DELIVERY

School counselors should possess the knowledge, abilities, skills and attitudes necessary to deliver a school counseling program aligning with the ASCA National Model.

III-A: Knowledge

School counselors should articulate and demonstrate an understanding of:

III-A-1. The concept of a guidance curriculum

III-A-2. Counseling theories and techniques that work in school, such as solutionfocused brief counseling, reality therapy, cognitivebehavioral therapy

III-A-3. Counseling theories and techniques in different settings, such as individual planning, group counseling and classroom guidance

III-A-4. Classroom management

III-A-5. Principles of career planning and college admissions, including financial aid and athletic eligibility

III-A-6. Principles of working with various student populations based on ethnic and racial background, English language proficiency, special needs, religion, gender and income

III-A-7. Responsive services

III-A-8. Crisis counseling, including grief and bereavement

III-B: Abilities and Skills

An effective school counselor is able to accomplish measurable objectives demonstrating the following abilities and skills.

III-B-1. Implements the school guidance curriculum

III-B-1a. Crosswalks ASCA Student Competencies with appropriate guidance curriculum

III-B-1b. Develops and presents a developmental guidance curriculum addressing all students' needs, including closing-the-gap activities

III-B-1c. Demonstrates classroom management and instructional skills

III-B-1d. Develops materials and instructional strategies to meet student needs and school goals

III-B-1e. Encourages staff involvement to ensure the effective implementation of the school guidance curriculum

III-B-1f. Knows, understands and uses a variety of technology in the delivery of guidance curriculum activities

III-B-1g. Understands multicultural and pluralistic trends when developing and choosing guidance curriculum

III-B-1h. Understands the resources available for students with special needs

III-B-2. Facilitates individual student planning

III-B-2a. Understands individual student planning as a component of a comprehensive program.

III-B-2b. Develops strategies to implement individual student planning, such as strategies for appraisal, advisement, goalsetting, decision-making, social skills, transition or postsecondary planning

III-B-2c. Helps students establish goals, and develops and uses planning skills in collaboration with parents or guardians and school personnel

III-B-2d. Understands career opportunities, labor market trends, and global economics, and uses various career assessment techniques to assist students in understanding their abilities and career interests

III-B-2e. Helps students learn the importance of college and other postsecondary education and helps students navigate the college admissions process

III-B-2f. Understands the relationship of academic performance to the world of work, family life and community service

III-B-2g. Understands methods for helping students monitor and direct their own learning and personal/social and career development

III-B-3. Provides responsive services

III-B-3a. Understands how to make referrals to appropriate professionals when necessary

III-B-3b. Lists and describes interventions used in responsive services, such as consultation, individual and small-group counseling, crisis counseling, referrals and peer and substance abuse counseling, within a continuum of care

III-B-3m. Understands the role of the school counselor and the school counseling program in the school crisis plan

III-B-4 Implements system support activities for the comprehensive school counseling program

III-B-4a. Creates a system support planning document addressing school counselor's responsibilities for professional development, consultation and collaboration and program management

III-B-4b. Coordinates activities that establish, maintain and enhance the school counseling program as well as other educational programs

III-B-4c. Conducts in-service training for other stakeholders to share school counseling expertise

III-B-4d. Understands and knows how to provide supervision for school counseling interns consistent with the principles of the ASCA National Model

III-C: Attitudes

School counselors believe:

III-C-1 School counseling is one component in the continuum of care that should be available to all students

III-C-2 School counselors coordinate and facilitate counseling and other services to ensure all students receive the care they need, even though school counselors may not personally provide the care themselves

III-C-3 School counselors engage in developmental counseling and short-term responsive counseling

III-C-4 School counselors should refer students to district or community resources to meet more extensive needs such as long-term therapy or diagnoses of disorders

IV: MANAGEMENT

School counselors should possess the knowledge, abilities, skills and attitudes necessary to manage a school counseling program aligning with the ASCA National Model.

IV-A: Knowledge

School counselors should articulate and demonstrate an understanding of:

IV-A-1. Leadership principles, including sources of power and authority, and formal and informal leadership

IV-A-2. Organization theory to facilitate advocacy, collaboration and systemic change

IV-A-3. Presentation skills for programs such as teacher inservices and results reports to school boards

IV-A-4. Time management, including long- and short-term management using tools such as schedules and calendars IV-A-5. Data-driven decision making

IV-A-6. Current and emerging technologies such as use of the Internet, Web-based resources and management information systems

IV-B: Abilities and Skills

An effective school counselor is able to accomplish measurable objectives demonstrating the following abilities and skills.

IV-B-1. Negotiates with the administrator to define the management system for the comprehensive school counseling program

IV-B-1a. Discusses and develops the components of the school counselor management system with the other members of the counseling staff

IV-B-1b. Presents the school counseling management system to the principal, and finalizes an annual school counseling management agreement

IV-B-1c. Discusses the anticipated program results when implementing the action plans for the school year

IV-B-1d. Participates in professional organizations

IV-B-1e. Develops a yearly professional development plan demonstrating how the school counselor advances relevant knowledge, skills and dispositions

IVB-1f. Communicates effective goals and benchmarks for meeting and exceeding expectations consistent with the administrator-counselor agreement and district performance appraisals

IV-B-1g. Uses personal reflection, consultation and supervision to promote professional growth and development

IV-B-2. Establishes and convenes an advisory council for the comprehensive school counseling program

IV-B-2a. Uses leadership skills to facilitate vision and positive change for the comprehensive school counseling program

IV-B-2b. Determines appropriate education stakeholders who should be represented on the advisory council

IV-B-2c. Develops meeting agendas

IV-B-2d. Reviews school data, school counseling program audit and school counseling program goals with the council

IV-B-2e. Records meeting notes and distributes as appropriate

IV-B-2f. Analyzes and incorporates feedback from advisory council related to school counseling program goals as appropriate

IV-B-3. Collects, analyzes and interprets relevant data, including process, perception and results data, to monitor and improve student behavior and achievement

IV-B-3a. Analyzes, synthesizes and disaggregates data to examine student outcomes and to identify and implement interventions as needed

IV-B-3b. Uses data to identify policies, practices and procedures leading to successes, systemic barriers and areas of weakness

IV-B-3c. Uses student data to demonstrate a need for systemic change in areas such as course enrollment patterns; equity and access; and the achievement, opportunity and information gap

IV-B-3d. Understands and uses data to establish goals and activities to close the achievement, opportunity and information gap

IV-B-3e. Knows how to use and analyze data to evaluate the school counseling program, research activity outcomes and identify gaps between and among different groups of students

IV-B-3f. Uses school data to identify and assist individual students who do not perform at grade level and do not have opportunities and resources to be successful in school

IV-B-3g. Knows and understands theoretical and historical bases for assessment techniques

IV-B-4. Organizes and manages time to implement an effective school counseling program

IV-B-4a. Identifies appropriate distribution of school counselor's time based on delivery system and school's data

IV-B-4b. Creates a rationale for school counselor's time to focus on the goals of the comprehensive school counseling program

IV-B-4c. Identifies and evaluates fairshare responsibilities, which articulate appropriate and inappropriate counseling and non-counseling activities

IV-B-4d. Creates a rationale for the school counselor's total time spent in each component of the school counseling program

IV-B-5. Develops calendars to ensure the effective implementation of the school counseling program

IV-B-5a. Creates annual, monthly and weekly calendars to plan activities to reflect school goals

IV-B-5b. Demonstrates time management skills including scheduling, publicizing and prioritizing time and task

IV-B-6. Designs and implements action plans aligning with school and school counseling program goals

IV-B-6a. Uses appropriate academic and behavioral data to develop guidance curriculum and closing-the-gap action plan and determines appropriate students for the target group or interventions

IV-B-6b. Identifies ASCA domains, standards and competencies being addressed by the plan

IV-B-6c. Determines the intended impact on academics and behavior

IV-B-6d. Identifies appropriate activities to accomplish objectives

IV-B-6e. Identifies appropriate resources needed

IV-B-6f. Identifies data-collection strategies to gather process, perception and results data

IV-B-6g. Shares results of action plans with staff, parents and community.

IV-C: Attitudes

School counselors believe:

IV-C-1. A school counseling program and guidance department must be managed like other programs and departments in a school

IV-C-2. One of the critical responsibilities of a school counselor is to plan, organize, implement and evaluate a school counseling program

IV-C-3. Management of a school counseling program must be done in collaboration with administrators.

V: ACCOUNTABILITY

School counselors should possess the knowledge, abilities, skills and attitudes necessary to monitor and evaluate the processes and results of a school counseling program aligning with the ASCA National Model.

V-A: Knowledge
School counselors should articulate and demonstrate an understanding of:

V-A-1. Basic concept of results-based school counseling and accountability issues

V-A-2. Basic research and statistical concepts to read and conduct research

V-A-3. Use of data to evaluate program effectiveness and to determine program needs

V-A-4. Program audits and results reports

V-B: Abilities and Skills
An effective school counselor is able to accomplish measurable objectives demonstrating the following abilities and skills.

V-B-1. Uses data from results reports to evaluate program effectiveness and to determine program needs

V-B-1a. Uses formal and informal methods of program evaluation to design and modify comprehensive school counseling programs

V-B-1b. Uses student data to support decision making in designing effective school counseling programs and interventions

V-B-1c. Measures results attained from school guidance curriculum and closing-the-gap activities

V-B-1d. Works with members of the school counseling team and with the administration to decide how school counseling programs are evaluated and how results are shared

V-B-1e. Collects process, perception and results data

V-B-1f. Uses technology in conducting research and program evaluation

V-B-1g. Reports program results to professional school counseling community

V-B-1h. Uses data to demonstrate the value the school counseling program adds to student achievement

V-B-1i.   Uses results obtained for program improvement
V-B-2.   Understands and advocates for appropriate school counselor
           performance appraisal process based on school counselors com-
           petencies and compietion of the guidance curriculum and
           agreed-upon action plans
V-B-2a.   Conducts self-appraisal related to school counseling skills and
           performance
V-B-2b.   Identifies how school counseling activities fit within categories
           of performance appraisal instrument
V-B-2c.   Encourages administrators to use performance appraisal instru-
           ment reflecting appropriate responsibilities for school coun-
           selors
V-B-3.   Conducts a program audit
V-B-3a.   Completes a program audit to compare current school counsel-
           ing program implementation with the ASCA National Model
V-B-3b.   Shares the results of the program audit with administrators, the
           advisory council and other appropriate stakeholders
V-B-3c.   Identifies areas for improvement for the school counseling pro-
           gram

V-C: Attitudes

School counselors believe:
V-C-1.   School counseling programs should achieve demonstrable
           results
V-C-2.   School counselors should be accountable for the results of the
           school counseling program
V-C-3.   School counselors should use quantitative and qualitative data
           to evaluate their school counseling program and to demonstrate
           program results
V-C-4.   The results of the school counseling program should be ana-
           lyzed and presented in the context of the overall school and dis-
           trict performance

Counseling Competencies and Performance Indicators Assessment Criteria – State Sample

PERFORMANCE INDICATORS

A. PROMOTES STUDENT GROWTH AND PERFORMANCE.

A1. Plans activities consistent with state board rules and statutes that promote increased student achievement.

Explanation/Example(s) School counselors provide expertise to students, parents, staff, and stakeholders on student career planning, attendance policies, progress monitoring and grade recovery, student progression, promotion requirements, graduation requirements, TARGET, alternative education programs including dropout prevention programs, and Exceptional Education programs. School counselors provide information and direct services to students and parents for career and academic advisement, student career planning, attendance, and TARGET.

A2. Plans activities consistent with district policies, procedures, program standards, and district and school improvement plans that promote increased student achievement.

Explanation/Example(s) School counselors serve as a resource to the school's programs and efforts to increase student achievement through activities, such as: TARGET; classroom guidance and/or small group counseling on study skills, time management, organizational skills, goal setting, anger management, and interpersonal relationships; interventions to address behavior management and academic success; teacher consultation; and referrals to school and district safety nets and outside agencies as appropriate.

A3. Shows evidence of planning and implementing a data-driven comprehensive school counseling program.

Explanation/Example(s) The counselor works with the school leadership (i.e. school improvement team, shared decision making team, School Advisory Council, grade level or subject departments) and utilizes school data to identify areas of need that can be addressed through a comprehensive guidance program. The counselor uses many resources to address the identified needs, and maps out an annual plan for implementation of program. Indicators include a monthly guidance calendar; copies of memos to parents, administrators, and community detailing program activities. The counselor works with the leadership of the school to develop and implement guidance services based on an analysis of student data. The counselor uses the data to develop an action plan which addresses at least one of the three domains – academic, career, and personal/social – of the ASCA National Standards for School Counseling. To evaluate the action plan the counselor produces a results report.

A4. Demonstrates understanding of equity/inclusion for under-represented students in rigorous course work

Explanation/Example(s) The counselor demonstrates efforts to assure that all students have access to rigorous course work by closely working with administration involved in class scheduling and class assignments to raise awareness of inequitable practices. The counselor seeks and utilizes all available student information when assisting students with goal setting, such as grades and GPA, cumulative records, test scores, and interest inventories. The counselor encourages students to take courses not traditional to their gender, race, disability, or ethnicity if the student shows interest in one of those areas (e.g. math and science for girls, early childhood education for boys.)

A5. Provides consultation to parents and teachers with regard to meeting needs of students, and assists in the formulation of instructional support strategies

Explanation/Example(s) The counselor builds consultation time into a daily posted schedule with the understanding that consultation can also be done on an as needed basis. The focus of consultation is to work collaboratively with the parent and/or teacher to plan appropriate strategies to meet the needs of students. The counselor works closely with teachers, parents, and students to provide input in planning instructional strategies that are appropriate for the needs of the individual student and/or classroom.

B. DEMONSTRATES THE ABILITY TO PLAN AND DELIVER GUIDANCE SERVICES.

B1. Makes effective use of time

Explanation/Example(s) The counselor keeps a calendar/daily log reflecting time allotment for guidance activities, i.e. classroom guidance, group counseling, parent conferences, observations of students, individual counseling, staff consultation, child study team activities, etc. The counselor strives to balance his/her time commitments so as not to compromise the provision of guidance services.

B2. Shows evidence of flexible procedures

Explanation/Example(s) The counselor strives to be available to deal with immediate needs and/or crisis situations and adjusts schedule accordingly. The counselor utilizes feedback from students, staff, parents, and administrators to assure that services are timely and essential.

B3. Uses supplemental materials to enhance guidance services

Explanation/Example(s) The counselor accesses resources such as *Implementing National Counseling Standards: A Resource Guide, Florida Counseling for Future Education Handbook, The American School Counseling Association (ASCA) National Model: A Framework for School Counseling Programs, The ASCA National Standards for School Counseling Programs, High School Counselors Handbook*, and other related materials to plan an effective guidance program.

B4. Demonstrates knowledge of availability of community resources

Explanation/Example(s) The counselor maintains a current community resource guide, (e.g. the Directory of Human Services,) which is readily accessible when needed.

B5. Uses technology for monitoring student progress, student career/academic planning, acquiring and accessing data needed to inform decision making of individual students and whole school

Explanation/Example(s) The counselor is able to access school data that is published on the district web site. The counselor utilizes reports from SIMS and Research and Evaluation to obtain information on individual students to assist in decision-making. The counselor uses such websites at Florida Bright Futures, Facts.org, Florida Student Financial Aid, and College Board Florida Partnership to assist students with career and academic planning (secondary counselors).

B6. Selects appropriate classroom guidance activities

Explanation/Example(s) The counselor selects classroom guidance activities that are aligned with the school's mission, school improvement plan goals, and an analysis of school data. The counselor may also conduct a needs assessment among faculty, students, and parents to determine appropriate classroom guidance activities.

B7. Uses evaluative information for program improvement

Explanation/Example(s) The counselor uses evaluation instruments such as pre- and post-test assessments, surveys, and questionnaires to determine the effectiveness of the counseling program. This information is used to make any adjustments to the program during the process of ongoing evaluation.

C. DEMONSTRATES KNOWLEDGE OF COUNSELING TECHNIQUES AND STUDENT DEVELOPMENT.

C1. Demonstrates multi-cultural and cross-cultural sensitivity

Explanation/Example(s) The counselor uses materials with non-biased language, representing a cross section of different cultures and nationalities; treats all individuals fairly regardless of sex or ethnicity; adjusts interactions to accommodate the verbal and nonverbal language patterns of different ethnic and racial groups; holds all students to high expectations and assists students in accessing resources and opportunities necessary for success.

C2. Utilizes counselor techniques that are sound, appropriate, and research- or experientially based

Explanation/Example(s) The counselor utilizes techniques such as brief counseling that are better suited to the school environment than traditional approaches.

C3. Exhibits knowledge of child growth and development, including learning styles

Explanation/Example(s) The counselor assists faculty and students in understanding how students learn in different ways. The counselor utilizes knowledge of child developmental stages to recommend intervention strategies that are appropriate. The counselor encourages faculty to take this information into account when evaluating students.

C4. Keeps abreast of and utilizes current guidance and counseling developments and techniques

Explanation/Example(s) The counselor attends workshops and reads professional journals to maintain current knowledge of counseling developments and techniques.

D. DEMONSTRATES THE ABILITY TO UTILIZE GROUP MANAGEMENT TECHNIQUES.

D1. Uses time effectively

Explanation/Example(s) The counselor allots adequate time for group activities and does not over dwell in presentation, interaction, or questioning. Attention is given to allowing sufficient time for learning rather than hurrying through the activity.

D2. Specifies expectations for group behavior

Explanation/Example(s) The counselor explains expectations of behavior and gives reasons for students to behave in certain ways. Appropriate student behavior may indicate that expectations have been made clear. However, if an inappropriate behavior occurs without subsequent statement or clarification of expectations, no credit should be given. Inappropriate behavior is characterized by its inconsistency with accepted norms or counselor expectations. The definitions of appropriate behavior vary with the context of the activity. Common inappropriate behavior includes off-task behavior, noisy call outs, and misuse of equipment.

D3. Encourages active participation

Explanation/Example(s) The counselor pursues student contributions, demonstrations, and questions with a frequency appropriate to the activity. The counselor may prompt, rephrase, and call on non-volunteers to increase student participation.

D4. Maintains momentum of presentation

Explanation/Example(s) The counselor maintains momentum by staying on the topic in counselor-centered activities, and does not interrupt activities unnecessarily. Focus can also be lost through delays, unnecessary digressions, and lengthy transitions. The majority of students are engaged in learning activities through the group activity.

D5. Provides feedback that is constructive

Explanation/Example(s) The counselor offers specific feedback to individuals and/or the group which reinforces those aspects of behavior which are acceptable. The counselor encourages group participation by establishing a climate that is non-threatening and inviting.

D6. Demonstrates non-verbal behavior that shows interest

Explanation/Example(s) The counselor relates to students in a pleasant manner by using students' names, making eye contact, smiling, exhibiting appropriate facial expressions, using appropriate gestures, and using a positive tone of voice.

E. SHOWS SENSITIVITY TO STUDENT NEEDS BY MAINTAINING A POSITIVE SCHOOL CLIMATE.

E1. Establishes/maintains rapport with students

Explanation/Example(s) The counselor attempts to maintain a positive atmosphere by making eye contact with students, smiling, using a positive tone of voice, and calling students by name. The counselor acknowledges the presence of students with positive remarks or questions. Communication with students has an absence of sarcasm, harsh criticism, or condescension.

E2. Establishes climate of courtesy and respect
Explanation/Example(s) The counselor maintains a climate of respect between the student and the counselor by encouraging student input, achievement, and effort. The counselor listens attentively to student remarks, acknowledging ideas or opinions positively whenever possible. The counselor displays regard for student questions by answering promptly or giving an appropriate deferment. The counselor praises, by word or deed, student effort as well as student achievement.

E3. Holds reasonable expectations for student social/academic behavior
Explanation/Example(s) The counselor maintains appropriate and consistent expectations for behavior and academic progress. There is evidence that students are informed about classroom or group rules. The counselor treats students fairly and consistently while attempting to balance student individuality in ability and background.

E4. Demonstrates enthusiasm for student performance or involvement
Explanation/Example(s) The counselor displays enthusiasm for school activities and student involvement. A positive regard for school activities may be evidenced by the counselor's expressing interest in the student's involvement in clubs, sports, or other activities, and/or the counselor's participation in extra curricular activities.

E5. Instructs students in goal setting, problem solving, and connecting choices, behaviors, and outcomes.
Explanation/Example(s) The counselor recognizes the importance of the successful school experience for students. The counselor communicates an attitude of confidence in the students and their potential. Students are encouraged to set goals, work diligently, and persevere. The counselor supports appropriate social and academic behavior by providing students with the skills to problem solve and identify alternatives for positive consequences. The counselor helps students make the connection between choices, behaviors, and outcomes.

E6. Treats all students fairly

Explanation/Example(s) Personal regard for students is communicated by the counselor through the use of courtesy in interaction with the students. The counselor creates an environment in which all students are treated equitably.

F. DEMONSTRATES ABILITY TO COMMUNICATE EFFECTIVELY WITH STAKEHOLDERS.

F1. Is readily accessible to students, teachers, parents, and administrators

Explanation/Example(s) The counselor creates an environment of accessibility by implementing a system of communication which allows individuals many avenues with which to interact with the counselor.

F2. Shares information with students, teachers, parents, and administrators through individual consultation, presentations, and supplementary materials

Explanation/Example(s) The counselor is skilled in effective communication with varied groups and seeks opportunities to provide information essential to student success. The counselor provides many resources to the school community and is frequently sought for his/her expertise. Indicators may include in-service presentations to faculty; development of brochures and/or flyers providing helpful information to parents; written communication to teachers.

F3. Facilitates communication among students, parents, school personnel and community resources

Explanation/Example(s) The counselor works to build rapport with individuals before serious communication begins; works patiently with parents for whom schools may have threatening connotations; avoids joining in on conversations that demean parents; assists parents in obtaining needed services for their children through a referral and follow-up process and serves as liaison between the school and community agencies so that they may collaborate in efforts to help students.

F4. Uses effective and correct oral and written communications

Explanation/Example(s) The counselor exhibits oral communication without grammatical errors. Typical errors are 1) use of double negatives, 2) lack of subject-verb agreement, 3) incorrect verb tense, and 4) incorrect pronoun reference. Two or more errors are cause for denying credit.

Written communications initiated by the counselor may be considered to determine whether this indicator has been adequately demonstrated.

F5. Demonstrates social advocacy skills, i.e., effective voice in challenging the status quo in systems where inequities impede students' academic success

Explanation/Example(s) The counselor works to close the information gap by providing students with critical, timely information about college and career opportunities; works to increase the number of low socioeconomic status students and students of color who enroll in rigorous coursework; uses data to make informed decisions where change is needed in the system; works with teachers to develop strategies, programs (e.g. tutoring, mentoring) that address academic needs of students.

F6. Responds promptly and appropriately to parental concerns

Explanation/Example(s) The counselor responds to concerns expressed by parents in a timely and professional manner. Written documentation should be maintained by the counselor in order to provide record of the communication. Evidence of this indicator might include phone logs, notes, or conference logs.

G. DEMONSTRATES WILLINGNESS TO ASSUME GENERAL PROFESSIONAL RESPONSIBILITIES.

G1. Adheres to school and district policy

Explanation/Example(s) The counselor is aware of and conforms to school and district rules.

G2. Maintains accurate records

Explanation/Example(s) The counselor's records including plans for small groups and classroom guidance, log of individual counseling sessions, student attendance in small group counseling sessions, child study team documentation, individual achievement test results, are neat and accurate.

G3. Initiates and conducts parent-teachers conferences to report student progress according to school board policy

Explanation/Example(s) The counselor initiates, conducts, and/or participates in parent conferences to report student progress according to school board policy. The counselor should facilitate parents' access to student grades, work, portfolios, or whatever documentation is available to provide evidence of student progress.

G4. Exercises due care of equipment under his/her care

Explanation/Example(s) The counselor exercises appropriate care of equipment assigned to him/her. Equipment is returned in a condition similar to that which existed when assigned.

H. DEMONSTRATES A COMMITMENT TO PROFESSIONAL GROWTH.

H1. Continues to pursue professional growth and development through workshops, seminars, college coursework, and/or other professional activities

Explanation/Example(s) Indicators may include: Participating in staff development through development activities to enhance counseling skills; continuing growth through self-evaluation, study, and travel; participating in conferences, workshops, and professional organizations; using creative ideas from books, professional journals, and professional organizations; working toward an advanced degree; and seeking national board certification.

H2. Participates in school and/or district committees

Explanation/Example(s) The counselor actively participates in school and system-wide activities and actively participates on school and/or district committees. Activities may include: The counselor volunteering to participate in extra-curricular activities; sponsoring clubs and/or organizations; working cooperatively with administration in dealing with extra-curricular assignments; and lending support to staff members who are involved with extracurricular activities (i.e. hospitality committee, attend science fair, help sessions.)

I. SHOWS EVIDENCE OF PROFESSIONAL CHARACTERISTICS.

I1. Demonstrates initiative and assumes responsibility

Explanation/Example(s) The counselor identifies barriers to student success and actively implements programs and services to address those barriers; assumes leadership in identifying resources and safety nets.

I2. Demonstrates behaviors reflecting dignity and worth of people

Explanation/Example(s) The counselor attempts to maintain positive relationships at all times. He/She relates to individuals in a pleasant manner and secures cooperation from the them, makes eye contact, smiles, uses a positive tone of voice and demonstrates patience and kindness. All interactions with students, parents, and faculty model courtesy. The counselor avoids sarcasm and negative criticism, establishes a climate of courtesy and respect, encourages slow and reluctant students. Establishes and maintains positive rapport.

I3. Exercises good judgment
Explanation/Example(s) The counselor demonstrates a professional demeanor at all times. Provides a positive role model for students. Effectively communicates with other people. Gathers information relative to professional problems in order to make knowledge-based decisions. Practices appropriate problem solving techniques. Deals positively and objectively with professionally related problems.

I4. Maintains confidentiality
Explanation/Example(s) The counselor maintains appropriate confidentiality in his/her interactions with parents, students, teachers, administration, district staff, and community resources. Communicates at a professional level relative to school-related information.

I5. Maintains good attendance
Explanation/Example(s) The counselor maintains attendance that adheres to the contractual policies of the Duval County School Board (i.e. does not abuse personal leave, provides a doctor's statement as needed, uses sick leave for authorized purposes only.) Evidence of this indicator might include copies of leave forms and/or sign-in sheets.

I6. Is punctual
Explanation/Example(s) The counselor adheres to the established school hours on a regular basis, is punctual to meetings, classes, duties, and is prompt in submitting reports. Sign-in sheets, copies of reports that were turned in on time, and statements from administrative staff or others that the counselor is punctual in the accomplishment of assigned duties/responsibilities may be used to demonstrate this indicator.

I7. Maintains professional appearance
Explanation/Example(s) The counselor dresses appropriately for his/her role, maintains a proper appearance in conjunction with the accepted style of the day, and exhibits cleanliness and good grooming (refer to contract language.)

I8. Exercises emotional self-control
Explanation/Example(s) The counselor conducts school business in a professional manner; demonstrates emotional restraint when dealing with

students, parents, and co-workers; and promotes calm during emotional situations.

I9. Accepts evaluation and redirection and makes necessary changes or adjustments

Explanation/Example(s) The counselor accepts constructive criticism and redirection; recognizes weaknesses and seeks help voluntarily; demonstrates willingness and desire to improve; and shows evidence of implementing suggested changes and/or adjustments.

I10. Acts as student advocate

Explanation/Example(s) The counselor's first priority is to act in the best interest of the student. In situations where the counselor is aware that an individual and/or the institution may not be acting in the best interest of the student, the counselor makes this concern known to the appropriate personnel and collaboratively works to implement changes as deemed necessary.

Selection of these competencies was guided by findings of a review of validated assessment system and a review of the research.
Duval County Public Schools, Jacksonville, FL. Used with permission.

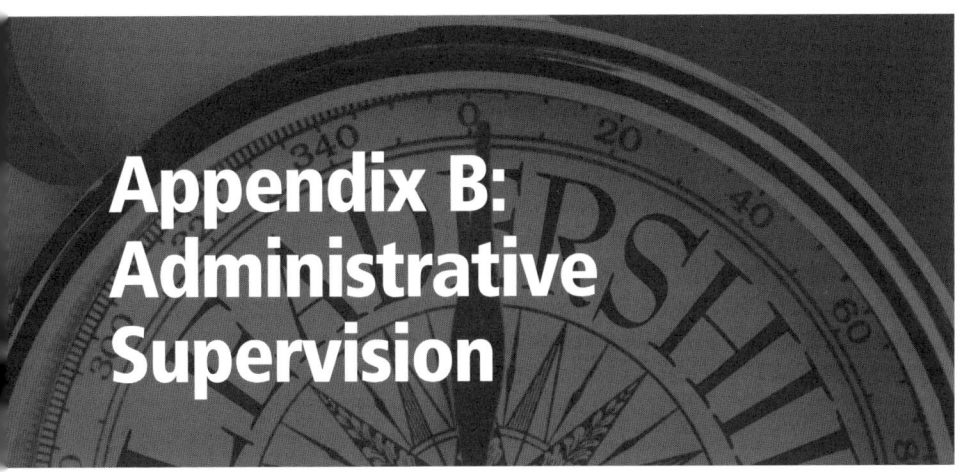

Appendix B: Administrative Supervision

School Counselor Assessment Instrument (SCAI) – Part A (State Sample)

(Rev. 7/08)

Counselor _____

PIN#_____RC#_____

School_____

Observer_____Date _____

Directions: The SCAI Part A is to be used for observation of thirty minutes or more. The TAI Part B is for documenting all other competencies. Place a check by the indicator number when the behavior is observed. Use the Comments/Recommendations space for descriptive notes.

Observation time: Start_____End_____

A. PROMOTES STUDENT GROWTH AND PERFORMANCE

**Comments/
Recommendations**   **Indicators**

____1. Plans activities consistent with state board rules and statutes that promote increased student achievement.

____2. Plans activities consistent with district policies, procedures, program standards, and district and school improvement plans that promote increased student achievement.

___3. Shows evidence of planning and implementing a data-driven comprehensive school counseling program.

___4. Demonstrates understanding of equity/inclusion for under-represented students in rigorous course work.

___5. Provides consultation to parents and teachers with regard to meeting needs of students, and assists in the formulation of instructional support strategies.

B. DEMONSTRATES THE ABILITY TO PLAN AND DELIVER GUIDANCE SERVICES

**Comments/
Recommendations**   **Indicators**

___1. Makes effective use of time.

___2. Shows evidence of flexible procedures.

___3. Uses supplemental materials to enhance guidance services.

___4. Demonstrates knowledge of availability of community resources.

___5. Uses technology for monitoring student progress, student career/academic planning, acquiring and accessing data needed to inform decision making of individual students and whole school.

___6. Selects appropriate classroom guidance activities.

___7. Uses evaluative information for program improvement.

C. DEMONSTRATES KNOWLEDGE OF COUNSELING TECHNIQUES AND STUDENT DEVELOPMENT

**Comments/
Recommendations**   **Indicators**

___1. Demonstrates multi-cultural and cross-cultural sensitivity.

___2. Utilizes counselor techniques that are sound, appropriate, and research- or experientially-based.

    ___3. Exhibits knowledge of child growth and development, including learning styles.

    ___4. Keeps abreast of and utilizes current guidance and counseling developments and techniques.

D. DEMONSTRATES THE ABILITY TO UTILIZE GROUP MANAGEMENT TECHNIQUES

**Comments/
Recommendations**   **Indicators**

    ___1. Uses time effectively.

    ___2. Specifies expectations for group behavior.

    ___3. Encourages active participation.

    ___4. Maintains momentum of presentation.

    ___5. Provides feedback that is constructive.

    ___6. Demonstrates non-verbal behavior that shows interest.

E. SHOWS SENSITIVITY TO STUDENT NEEDS BY MAINTAINING A POSITIVE SCHOOL CLIMATE

**Comments/
Recommendations**   **Indicators**

    ___1. Establishes/maintains rapport with students.

    ___2. Establishes climate of courtesy and respect.

    ___3. Holds reasonable expectations for student social/academic behavior.

    ___4. Demonstrates enthusiasm for student performance or involvement.

    ___5. Instructs students in goal setting, problem solving, and connecting choices, behaviors, and outcomes.

    ___6. Treats all students fairly.

School Counselor Assessment Instrument (SCAI) cont'd – Part B

(Rev 7/08)

Counselor _____Date_____

F. DEMONSTRATES ABILITY TO COMMUNICATE EFFECTIVELY

**Comments/
Recommendations**   **Indicators**

___1. Is readily accessible to students, teachers, parents, and administrators.

___2. Shares information with students, teachers, parents, and administrators through individual consultation, presentations, and supplementary materials.

___3. Facilitates communication among students, parents, school personnel and community resources.

___4. Uses effective and correct oral and written communications.

___5. Demonstrates social advocacy skills, i.e., effective voice in challenging the status quo in systems where inequities impede students' academic success.

___6. Responds promptly and appropriately to parental concerns.

G. DEMONSTRATES WILLINGNESS TO ASSUME GENERAL PROFESSIONAL RESPONSIBILITIES

**Comments/
Recommendations**   **Indicators**

___1. Adheres to school and district policy.

___2. Maintains accurate records.

___3. Initiates and conducts parent-teachers conferences to report student progress according to school board policy.

___4. Exercises due care of equipment under his/her care.

H. DEMONSTRATES A COMMITMENT TO PROFESSIONAL GROWTH

**Comments/
Recommendations**   **Indicators**

___1. Continues to pursue professional growth and development through workshops, seminars, college course work, and/or other professional activities.

___2. Participates in school and/or district committees.

I. SHOWS EVIDENCE OF PROFESSIONAL CHARACTERISTICS

**Comments/
Recommendations**   **Indicators**

___1. Demonstrates initiative and assumes responsibility.

___2. Demonstrates behaviors reflecting dignity and worth of people.

___3. Exercises good judgement.

___4. Maintains confidentiality.

___5. Maintains good attendance.

___6. Is punctual.

___7. Maintains professional appearance.

___8. Exercises emotional self-control.

___9. Accepts evaluation and redirection and makes necessary changes or adjustments.

__10. Acts as student advocate.

*Post-observation conference must be scheduled with 5 days of observation.

At this time all competencies are satisfactory EXCEPT the following circled competencies

A   B   C   D   E   F   G   H   I

**Only an unsatisfactory rating will result in reduction points.
The reduction points are as follows**
Competency A: -3 points; Competencies B through E: -2 points,
Competencies F through I: -1 point. Four or more reduction points
remains as an overall unsatisfactory evaluation.

Signature of Reviewer/Date   Signature of Counselor/Date

Annual Assessment for School Counselors k-12 Public Schools
Duval County Public Schools, Jacksonville, FL. Used with permission.

Acknowledgements

We extend our appreciation to the many students and colleagues who inspired us to write this book. Thank you to University of Massachusetts Boston graduate students Matthew Smith, Laura Fratangelo and Natalie Coady for help with library research. A special thank you to Kathleen Rakestraw of ASCA for her assistance in preparing the manuscript for publication.

About the Authors

Felicia L. Wilczenski, Ed.D. is professor and associate dean in the Graduate College of Education at the University of Massachusetts Boston. Her professional and research interests are applications of service-learning in school counselor education and professional development through mentoring.

Rebecca A. Schumacher, Ed.D. is a school counselor educator formerly with the University of Massachusetts Boston. Her professional and research interests are group work in schools, supervision and preparation of school counselors.

Amy Cook, Ph.D. is a faculty member in the school counseling program at the University of Massachusetts Boston. She supervises school counseling graduate students during practicum and internship. Her research interests are multicultural issues and counselor-educator preparation as well as examining ways to eliminate the achievement gap for English-language learners.